D0873502

ONLY THE NAMES HAVE CHANGED

JASON MACIOGE

AND

DAVE KATZOFF

GADD & COMPANY PUBLISHERS, INC.
A Division of The North River Press

The characters and events in this book are fictitious. Any similarity to real persons, living or dead, is coincidental and not intended by the author.

Gadd & Company Publishers, Inc.
A Division of The North River Press Publishing Corporation
79 Boice Road
Egremont, MA 01230
(413) 528-8895
Visit our website at www.gaddbooks.com

Printed in the United States of America
ISBN: 978-0-88427-910-5

for Bubba:
my beautiful basset hound
and best friend
&
for Howard Stern:
the king of all media; always the
gentleman; one of my heroes

ONLY THE NAMES
HAVE CHANGED

CHAPTER 1

A warm September rain pelts the windshield of a Buckingham Blue Range Rover Sport as it exits Kennedy Airport and gracefully hydroplanes westward. With the cruise control set at sixty-eight miles per hour, Jay Gordon finesses the gas pedal with his flip-flop just enough to maintain control of the vehicle's velocity.

"Can you even see out the back?"

Smitty is the lone human passenger. Jay glances into the rear view mirror. In the backseat, Axl, a tough and cuddly basset hound, shakes himself vigorously. Smitty groans.

"Your dog smells like ass, dude."

"I'd get used to it, my friend." Jay increases pressure on the accelerator and Smitty reclines his seat. The motorized hum rouses Axl, who barks curiously. Jay shushes his dog.

"Ah, listen… Do you hear that?"

"Hear what?" Smitty has allowed his eyes to droop shut.

"Exactly," Jay gloats. "Three hundred

horses and not a fuckin' sound."

"You should've went with the Cayenne," Smitty mutters without lifting his head.

Jay rolls his eyes.

"Porsche trucks are for guys who wear neck warmers and listen to trance."

Smitty finds this comical.

"Jay fuckin' Gordon!" His head wobbles sluggishly to the right.

Jay pushes the *resume* button on the steering wheel, and the Range Rover kicks back into auto-drive. "It's good to see you, Smit."

§   §   §

Jay and Walter "Smitty" Smith III met at boarding school when they were both seventeen. Smitty had been "extradited" from Trinity Catholic in Newton, Massachusetts, for selling cocaine to a seminarian study group. It was his third offense in as many years and even though his father was on the school board, the three-strike law took precedence. In the greater Boston area, private high schools operate like newspaper tabloids when it comes to exposing "code of conduct" scandals. Peddling "California Cornflakes" in each of his first three years made Walter Smith the Tony Montana of New England preparatory scholars. Every dean from Braintree to Weston knew his name, and despite a distinguished academic record and influential family ties, his reputation for gross delinquency was notorious.

His father, R.W., was a corporate lawyer, and his mother, Maureen, a partner at a public relations firm whose clients included state senators and congressmen from both sides of the aisle. The felony drug charges were eventually expunged from his record, but no private school within fifty miles was willing to accept Walter. So he landed at Mount Hermon Academy, a tame, rural boarding school situated in the northern valley of western Massachusetts. As a junior, he boarded with a surly, redheaded chap named Charlie McGurdy, who was notorious for masturbating while his roommate was still awake.

Smitty and Charlie did not last long as cohabitants. One night early into their second week, Charlie was furiously pleasuring himself under the covers when Smitty snapped. Without giving any forewarning, he pounced onto the adjacent bed and pummeled Charlie until his fists were sore. Earlier that day he had snuck off campus to buy a thirty-pack of Milwaukee's Best using a fake ID, and then bribed the man restocking the soda machine in the dorm lobby to fill the diet Sprite slot with beer cans. When the house parent burst into their room to investigate the clamor, he found Smitty sitting on his bed in his boxers and a bloody V-neck undershirt, casually sipping a cold brew.

Although MHA was a relatively small institution, it was socially governed by a subculture of stoners. Unlike Smitty, Jay Gordon kept his extracurricular delinquencies quiet. He was a solid B student and a decent, three-sport athlete, but on campus his most renowned attribute was his judicious troublemaking. Amongst his peers, he was widely considered the savviest and luckiest man to ever venture outside the parameters of school policy or civic law. His roommate, Colin, whose family owned a ski cabin in northern Vermont, got his driver's license early junior year and they began making trips to Burlington, returning with vacuum-sealed turkey bags full of fresh purple ganja.

Smitty and Jay started hanging out after the Charlie incident. Jay found the whole ordeal particularly amusing because he had also roomed with Charlie for half of his freshman year. Smitty's punishment was more like a perk. He was isolated to a single room on the east wing of the Chapman dormitory. Jay and Colin lived four doors down, and on most weeknights they would rendezvous after lights-out. The three of them would sit around the window ledge, smoking from Smitty's handblown glass water pipe, using otherwise neglected dryer sheets stuffed inside empty paper towel tubes to mask the smell of bubbler-hits.

§   §   §

The Range Rover staggers to a crawl as Jay taps the brakes with the affect of a drummer in an allegro crescendo. The rain has let up, but the windshield wipers still motor at a lively pace. Smitty senses the change in speed and blinks his eyes a few times before sitting up in his seat.

"Fuck, I forgot to get EZPass," Jay grumbles to himself as he digs for his wallet. Traffic for the Midtown Tunnel has begun well before the tollbooths, and a galaxy of red brake lights glistens in the raindrops on the foggy windshield. As they inch closer, Manhattan's eastside skyline emerges from the mist.

"There she is, the Big fucking wormy Apple." Smitty hands Jay a twenty-dollar bill. "My blood pressure rises at the very sight of this town. I don't know how people live here."

Jay seems slightly impatient. "You have a good flight?"

"Man, I hate those goddamn choppy charters. Boston to New York has got to be one of the worst short hauls in air travel."

"How are the folks?"

"The old man's got a four handicap now."

"Damn. That's close to scratch."

"Fuckin' right. He smoked my ass at Brookline CC yesterday."

Jay buries a smile beneath his jaw.

"But fuck, dude," Smitty gripes, "they live in Hilton Head most of the year. Only thing to *do* down there is play golf and eat saltwater taffy."

Smitty yawns as Jay lowers the air conditioning.

"What about Maureen? She retired yet?"

"Mom got her gold watch almost ten years ago. Damn, Gordy. Has it been that long?"

§ § §

Jay graduated from Cornell in 1992 and Smitty finished at Brown on the five-year-plus plan roughly eighteen months later. Both moved back to their hometowns in Massachusetts. Jay grew up in Lenox, a scenic township tucked inside the low-rise mountains of Berkshire County. He began working in the service industry as a waiter and bartender, and eventually floor manager. Lenox, where the regional high school team is called the Millionaires, is a community of sprawling estates, celebrated museums, and world-renowned theater companies. During the summer, the expansive grounds of Tanglewood are home to the Boston Symphony Orchestra and legendary concerts like James Taylor and Tony Bennett. Even for an Ivy League grad, working in the restaurant business in Lenox was a semi-reputable occupation out of college. In the Berkshires, some of the true-blooded natives regard themselves as more bucolic than Norman Rockwell's depiction of friendly New England villagers, but even the rural roughnecks consider Lenox "the pearl oyster" of the county.

Smitty grew up in a three-story brownstone in Brookline, an urbanized suburb on the periphery of Boston proper. Each summer since he was a toddler, the Smiths would take a weeklong trip to Berkshire County to watch the BSO perform. They stayed at Blantyre, a sumptuous country house hotel located a few miles east of Tanglewood. After Jay and Smitty met at MHA, those seven days in the Berkshires became the highlight of every subsequent summer. The Smiths and Gordons grew to be cordial acquaintances but "the boys" were virtually inseparable. They spent their days careening around Stockbridge Bowl on jet skis and motorboats, and at night they would drive twenty minutes south to Great Barrington and sneak into the bars with fake IDs.

When Smitty moved to San Diego, he severed virtually all of his East Coast ties. His older brother Luke had moved to Oregon, and his parents spent most of the year at their home in South Carolina. In the days before electronic mail, old-fashioned letter writing felt "too effeminate" for old boarding school chums (unless, of course, one of them was in prison). Email, however, offered men a more androgynous way of staying in touch. For nearly two years, Jay and Smitty communicated almost exclusively online, but when their emails trailed off, they stopped communicating altogether.

§ § §

As they pull up to the tollbooth, Jay lowers his window and the steamy, metropolitan humidity pours into the car.

"What's the best way to get to the Holland Tunnel?"

In a succinct motion, the toll collector waves his hand over his shoulder as if to say, "Keep going straight."

Smitty leans across the console and yells, "Thanks a lot, sir! You've been very helpful! Go Yankees! Bitch."

The commotion startles Axl, who lets out a deep-throated yelp.

"What a fuckin' douche!" Smitty has lost his composure. "Do we even know where the fuck we're—"

"Quit cursing around my fuckin' dog, asshole," Jay chides. "I can't *stand* driving in this city."

§   §   §

Throughout their twenties, Jay and Smitty shuffled through various jobs, apartments, houses, pets, and girlfriends, yet still managed to keep their friendship intact. Settled on opposite ends of the Mass Pike, they would arrange bi-monthly excursions or coordinate their vacation plans in Vermont or Nantucket, depending on the season. But as they approached their thirties, the pressures of success intensified, gradually dissolving their prep school commonalities. Smitty started a chain of moving and storage companies in eastern New England, and his business grew to be so profitable he expanded his operations to the West Coast. Jay opened a French bistro in Lenox and quickly parlayed his knowledge and revenue stream into other restaurant projects. More than three years passed without a word between them. Then, on a random Friday afternoon in the spring of 2003, Smitty called Jay with an announcement that eclipsed any lapse in friendship: he was getting married.

The following January, a day before the wedding, Jay sent a pair of steak knives and a bouquet of flowers to Smitty and his fiancée in California. He also sent a one-line email with no subject header:

Things are insane right now. I'll explain later. Sorry I can't be there. JG

Three years passed and finally Jay found an opportunity to make amends. He owned and managed two restaurants in Lenox—Maison, an upscale French bistro, and Ack's Pizza Shack, a surfer-themed eatery in the village square. He was also a managing partner at Porter's, a musky, New York-inspired steakhouse in Great Barrington. While raising cash through a private offering of his shell corporation, he was approached by a venture capitalist who saw potential in franchising his pizza restaurants in midwestern college towns and along the coast of California. Something inside him clicked. Two months later, Jay bought a brand new Range Rover and packed it with skis, golf clubs, a laptop, a small filing cabinet, and three weeks of travel gear. He dug up some tattered pillows and cashmere blankets and lined the backseat upholstery with a thick layer of cushioning for Axl. Then he called up his old buddy in San Diego.

§   §   §

"You don't want to stay in the city for the night, do you?"

"Hell, no," Smitty replies. "Let's see how far south we can get. My brother-in-law lives in Virginia Beach. I told him we were coming down and he wants to play nine holes tomorrow afternoon."

Jay lifts up the armrest on the console compartment, pulls out his iPod and plugs it into the MP3 jack.

"That's cool. I don't have anywhere to be."

After navigating through the maze of lower Manhattan, the collective mood of the travelers lightens. Smitty tilts his seat back slightly and Axl nestles himself in for another nap. Headed south on the New Jersey Turnpike, Jay returns to cruising mode.

"Oh! I almost forgot!" he reaches deep into the console and pulls out a Ziploc bag bursting with skunky ganja and a pack of orange Zig Zag rolling papers. Smitty's eyes light up.

"I can't even remember the last time I got blazed."

Jay nods. "Me neither. But this shit is some of that BC kush, and we're on a road trip, my friend."

§   §   §

Smitty held a bitter grudge for at least two years after the wedding. Many other friends from college and boarding school had attended, but Jay's absence, given how close they once were, bruised his ego badly. Jay knew this. He also knew that he owed Smitty an explanation, and franchising his restaurants out West became a convenient excuse to reunite. The whole adventure was intricately orchestrated. Jay simply needed the proper setting to divulge the last six years of his life and he knew the one thing Smitty would not turn down was an "old school" road trip.

§   §   §

Smitty uses the road atlas like a work desk, crafting an enormous, cone-shaped joint.

"It's just like riding a bike," Jay chuckles, knowing Smitty will realize this refers to more than just his craftsmanship with a Zig Zag rolling paper.

Jay reaches down to his iPod, and with one eye on the road, cues up a song.

"Might as well spark it. We got enough gas to get to Maryland."

He tilts open the smoking roof as Smitty touches the lighter to the tip of the conc and inhales long and deep. The piano intro to Night Ranger's "Sister Christian" softly tingles through the stereo speakers, and when Smitty hears the opening bars, he nearly chokes with laughter.

"Oh, wow!"

"Remember this one, Smit?" Jay reminisces gleefully. "This was the fucking *anthem* back in Chapman!"

They pass the cone back and forth for a while, each exhaling grayish yellow clouds and conjuring memories from nearly two decades ago. As the chorus approaches, they both pound the air drums and lip-synch the words:

"We're motorin'! What's your price for flight? In finding Mister Right. We'll be alright tonight."

Axl rattles his collar. He has never seen Jay smoke before and the sight of him exhaling vapors and gesticulating confuses him. But after about fifteen minutes, he settles into his own sedation. As the song ends, a deep, uncomfortable quiet fills the air.

After what feels like an hour, Jay's voice shatters the stillness.

"I'm sorry I missed the wedding, buddy." Smitty pauses before answering. "That's big of you to say."

"Seriously. I've felt bad about it for a while now."

Jay chooses his words carefully, but seems confident in his delivery.

"It was a tough time for me, bro. I'm not gonna sugarcoat it. I mean, business has been phenomenal, but I was put through the ringer for *years*."

Smitty nods. "You wanna talk about it?"

"It could take awhile."

"Alright, Gordy..." With exaggerated affect, he yanks his seat belt. "What was her name?" Smitty is not one for naïveté.

Jay smiles, but as he takes a long breath his lighthearted expression fades.

"Madison," he replies pensively.

CHAPTER 2

Leeland is a rural community in upstate New York, just east of Lake Oswego. Because of its proximity to the Canadian border, the local speech patterns combine a faint North Country inflection with a distinctive Nordic brogue. Town lore suggests that the accent comes from the drinking water, as do many of the human tendencies that are nurtured by the frigid climate and bleak topography. The seasons are less pronounced in Oswego County, as the cold months linger well into the spring, and autumn passes too quickly to be considered a season of its own. By Halloween, an insistent desolateness has regained its stronghold on the region. Each year, between November and May, Leelanders embrace and respect a culture of reclusion, as if Mother

Nature herself has implemented a curfew. In the Horn household, the winter months were prudently observed.

"You know there's nothing wrong with you, Madison," Jane Horn murmured.

Madison let out an unconvincing cough.

Without speaking, her mother went back to washing dishes and Maddy, as she was called, returned to her algebra homework at the breakfast bar. After the kitchen was cleaned, Jane turned off the overhead lights and sat idle at the bridge table by the window, staring out into the austere snowdrifts in the backyard.

§　§　§

From an early age, Maddy wholly rejected her community's seasonal routine. She played soccer, basketball, and softball year round, took piano lessons in the evenings, and participated in all the theater club productions. But as she grew older, she began to develop her own complex aversion to loneliness. By junior high, her body had matured quickly and visibly. She was the type of girl who garnered the interest of every boy at school, but only wanted to be noticed by her guidance counselor.

Around the time she was born, her father,

Bill, changed careers and joined the fraternity of life insurance salesman, dedicating the greater portion of his waking hours to managing a commission-based business. He spent six days a week cajoling people into purchasing life insurance products, and he brought home his extroverted mannerisms and unyielding positivity. Although he provided a comfortable lifestyle for his family, he never fully embraced the virtues of fatherhood beyond being the breadwinner. "Attitude determines altitude," he would always say, and he lived by this principle even when it did not apply. Jane mothered from the opposite end of the temperament spectrum, instilling her children with stern Christian values and a rigid sense of optimism. Taking on the role of homemaker, she labored neurotically around the house with a vacuum and a feather duster and was perpetually discontented. Her primary maternal duties were to see that her three boys were well taken care of, which left Madison with an obligatory sense of independence.

Jane Orwell met H. William Horn Jr. at a church picnic in the summer of 1960. His given name was Harry, but he went by Bill. He had recently graduated from Syracuse University and had returned to his native Leeland to begin a career as a city planner.

Jane was smitten by his wholesome demeanor and the comely blend of Brylcreem and Old Spice emanating from above his neck. The two dated very cordially at first, and after scores of romantic overtures, Bill finally convinced Jane to attend Sunday service in Leeland. Ten years later, they were married with three boys: Johnny, Jackie and Jerry.

On March 8, 1971, the night Muhammad Ali fought Joe Frazier at the old Madison Square Garden in New York City, Jane went into labor. She was rushed to St. Lawrence hospital and after an emergency C-section, gave birth to a little girl. In between visits to the maternity ward, Bill snuck into the waiting room to watch the fight. In 1971, America was divided by those who rooted for Muhammad Ali and those who rooted for Joe Frazier. The Horn family would refer to Ali only as Cassius Clay and they detested his luminary bravado and penchant for civil disobedience. They were staunch Frazier supporters, which spoke more to their political values than their affinity for the fighter. After a grueling and historic fifteen-round bout, Joe Frazier was declared the winner by decision. Bill and Jane celebrated by naming their only girl Madison, after the world's most famous arena.

"My stomach hurts," Maddy declared after a few minutes of silence.

Mrs. Horn had not moved from her seat. "Finish your homework, child," she murmured.

Maddy was undeterred. "Mom? Does Lenox High have a basketball team?"

"I don't know, Madison." Jane answered with a quivery voice.

Earlier that fall, Maddy noticed her father had hired landscapers to groom their property twice a month. She found this odd because Bill was not one to pay for cosmetics of any sort. Then she discovered the familiar "FOR SALE" sign staked in her front lawn; it was visible the moment her school bus turned onto her street. Seeing it for the first time infused her with the excitement of uncertainty. At supper that evening, Bill announced to his family that they were moving to Lenox, Massachusetts.

Her mother took it particularly hard. Aside from a few Sunday drives and a trip to Disney World when Maddy was five, Jane had never really left Oswego County. Like an indigenous field weed uprooted from its natural habitat, Mrs. Horn recoiled at the thought of being transplanted.

"I hope they don't talk funny in Lenox. I hate how people around here talk," Madison said.

"We talk just fine," snapped Jane indignantly. "You sound ignorant when you say things like that."

"People in Leeland are boring. They—" Jane interjected before Maddy could finish. "That's enough, Madison."

Shortly after Maddy's seventeenth birthday, the Horns relocated to Lenox. At the time, John was in college and Jackie had left home to work on a painting crew in Rochester, but Jerry and Maddy transferred to Lenox High mid-semester. Bill started his new job immediately, leaving Jane and the children to unpack and furnish the house. Jerry was exempt from housework, so Maddy helped her mother after school for two weeks until they were settled. In between basketball and softball seasons, Maddy had no after-school commitments, so she rode around on her mountain bike, carefully observing her new surroundings.

Springtime in the Berkshires blossomed with far more vivaciousness than she had ever seen before. People in the neighborhood were tending to their yards and gardens. Shopkeepers in town swept the sidewalks as if they were whisking winter away with push brooms. At the corner store on Church Street, she discovered a bin of penny candy and five-cent lollipops, and on most weekday afternoons, she could be spotted pedaling through the streets of Lenox with a sour apple Blow Pop in her mouth.

Diagonally across from where her parents lived, she saw a hand-carved sign posted in the front yard that read: Faith First Bible School. The logo was a bright gold cross, fully emerged from what looked like rosy red shrubbery. The writing was in old calligraphy, as if the font itself was lifted from the original scriptures. One Saturday morning in late spring, she was riding by and heard the sounds of children screeching and laughing in the backyard. This was the type of thing that almost never happened in Leeland until midsummer. Maddy was intrigued. She stopped and rested her bike on the sidewalk. Underneath the tall picket fence, she could see sneakers scampering back and forth and a soccer ball sliding through the grass. A man appeared in the shadows of the doorway at the adjacent house and he stepped outside to greet her. He was dressed in neatly pressed slacks and a white short-sleeve button-up. The emblem on his pocket matched the logo on the sign.

"Hiya, young lady." Not waiting for a response, he walked up and extended his hand. "I'm Gerry Stewart."

"Hi." Madison inched closer to her bike.

"Is that your family who moved in right

over there?" As he pointed, Maddy noticed the sweat stain underneath his armpit.

"Yeah. I'm Madison Horn. My brother's name is Jerry."

Once they began talking, Maddy warmed up to him. He told her that most of the kids at the school called him Pastor G and that on Saturday mornings they played an informal game of soccer after prayer group. He asked her if she would like to join in and she accepted without hesitation. Wheeling her bike onto the front stoop, he guided her through the house and past the mud porch that led to the backyard. As they walked down a long corridor, Maddy was wide-eyed. Backpacks and windbreakers were placed inside carefully marked cubbyholes. Cookies baking in the oven gave off an aroma of sweet coziness. The atmosphere was a stark contrast to her increasingly lonely home life. The adjacent lot housed a massive complex, which served as both a church and a bible school. Sunday services typically drew upwards of three hundred worshipers from all over the county. Behind the Stewarts' house, a small grass field was marked by two rickety soccer goals on each end. When they stepped outside, Pastor G interrupted the game to make an announcement.

"Brothers and sisters!" he exclaimed.

"This is Madison Horn. She's going to play with us today, so make sure the teams are even."

Maddy greeted the group with an awkward wave. The boys seemed suddenly self-conscious, but the girls were slightly more amicable, if apprehensive. Gerry stepped back inside to watch from the window as Maddy quickly dominated the game with her advanced footwork and powerful kicks.

Gerry "Pastor G" Stewart was an unctuously friendly man with a magnanimous bravado and a distinctive Dallas drawl. He wore his hair slicked back and his shirt tucked under his oval belt buckle, displaying his potbelly with the unabashed pride of a true Texan. A natural salesman, Gerry spoke in a simplistic vernacular and often prefaced his statements by referencing the word of God, which augmented the conviction in his voice. He was a man of two religions: football and the King James Bible, and on Sundays, church and sport were separated only by the time between his morning sermon and kick-off of the first game.

In a matter of weeks, the community of Faith First had embraced Maddy as one of their own. They provided her with the type of attention and familial affection she never received at home. During school days, Pastor G and his wife, Martha, taught classes to a group of students whose ages ranged from eleven to seventeen. Of the fifty pupils enrolled at Faith First Bible School, four were the Stewart's own children and three were cousins who had recently relocated to Lenox from Fort Worth. Maddy, who was a junior in high school, decided not to play softball for the Millionaires that spring, and instead attended a daily afternoon prayer group guided by Pastor G.

Gerry and Martha had twin boys and two girls. Steven and Jed were Maddy's age, and Karen and Alison were eight and ten, respectively. When Maddy joined the church, the twins engaged in a very restrained competition to impress her. Steven was more athletic and used his prowess to flirt with Maddy whenever they played sports as a group. Jed was a theocratic devotee and he would often ask Maddy to stay late and memorize passages with him.

By the time Lenox High adjourned for the summer, Maddy was spending all of her free time at Faith First. On occasion, she even skipped school to partake in special events. Bill and Jane knew very little of what went on across the street, but as partisan Christians they were inclined to encourage Maddy's affiliation with the Bible-centric organization. But gradually they began to notice a change in her demeanor and routine. For the first time, she had let her grades slip and stopped participating in organized sports. She no longer studied piano and lost interest in theater.

Martha and Gerry ordered her a brand new King James Bible, and when it arrived they presented it to her in front of the whole school. All the children applauded as if it were a rite of passage. Although Madison never read the Bible on her own time, she kept the book atop her bedside table as a constant reminder of her other family.

Every Fourth of July Pastor G would host a barbecue in the backyard, culminating after sunset in a low-level display of fireworks. All the children who attended school talked about it for weeks leading up to the holiday. Maddy had a proclivity for parties and barbecues, but a more tepid appreciation for pyrotechnics. At this year's celebration, she was asked to come over early and help set up. When she got there, it was as if the celebration was for her. On separate occasions, Steven and Jed told her how pretty she looked. Martha pulled her aside and whispered to her how happy they were to have her in their home. Karen and Alison made her cupcakes in their easy-bake oven and wrote Maddy's initials in frosting. Gerry's brother Rick and his three children arrived with a basket of gingerbread cookies and a colorful array of helium balloons. Maddy enjoyed the attention far too much to be distrusting. When the rest of the students arrived, everyone congregated in the chapel at the complex next door. After prayers, Maddy was asked to stay behind with Uncle Rick. Pastor G assured her that there was something very important he had to talk with her about. Albeit confused, Maddy obliged. Rick took her into the office behind the pews. Her heart began to race. He instructed her to sit down and take off her cardigan sweater so that she would be more comfortable.

"Today will be the most important day of your life," he said as he pulled out his Bible. Then he asked if she was ready.

Maddy gulped and nodded hesitantly. Uncle Rick opened his book and began reading passages that were underlined in red ink. Beads of sweat formed on her forehead. As he flipped through the pages, he would periodically lick his fingers, a habit her mother would surely consider unsanitary. Maddy's mind wandered but was careful not to let her eyes drift too far from Uncle Rick's vantage. Other than a framed glossy portrait of a blue-eyed Jesus in a white gown with a gold halo above his flowing mane, the walls were white and bare. In between recitations, Maddy could hear the electric hum of the fluorescent lights above her. Nearly thirty minutes passed and the purpose of this private sermon was still unclear. Finally, Rick asked for her hands and she timidly extended them. Claustrophobia and restlessness were beginning to take hold of her. Rick placed both of their hands on the Bible and then asked Maddy to repeat after him:

"I am now ready to accept Jesus Christ as my Lord and savior. I will follow His word wherever it may lead, and I will lead others to follow me. I now understand that my salvation is in His hands, and only He can offer mercy if He chooses. In Jesus' name I ask for these blessings... Together we pray."

Maddy noticed that Rick's eyes were closed and he was reciting passages he had committed to memory. Just before his last phrase, she abruptly shut hers so he would not notice that they had been open. After he finished, he lifted both of their hands off the book and grinned broadly.

"So, how do you feel?"

Maddy wiped her sweaty palms on her shorts and mustered a thankful smile. But she felt more befuddled than renewed.

"Are you ready to go greet your brothers and sisters in Christ?"

She was eager to leave that office.

"We are your family now, Madison. Anything you need, you can always come to any one of us."

As Maddy stepped out of the church, a line of people had formed, eager to greet her. Steven and Jed were at the front. They both hugged her bashfully. Then the rest of the children congratulated her and welcomed her to the "family." Lastly, Martha and Gerry were waiting. They both told her how proud they were to be her "parents," and how she touched each and every person in the congregation with her "spirit of joy." Maddy had never received such accolades from her own family.

By September, it had been six months and Maddy had no friends or social interactions beyond the insular walls of Faith First. Her brother Jerry had graduated from high school earlier that spring, and when summer ended he left home for college in Bridgewater. Since Madison was the only remaining child under their supervision, Bill and Jane decided to take a more active role in her life. They insisted she try out for the Lenox High soccer team, and although Maddy unequivocally rejected their authority, she seemed eager to play competitive sports again. However, the day before she received her varsity uniform, Pastor G persuaded her to stop playing because she was missing too many afternoon prayer groups. The Horns discovered their daughter had quit the team when they showed up at her first game and she was nowhere to be found.

Maddy's relationship with her family grew from strained to estranged. Since moving to Lenox, she had developed a defiant attitude toward her parents. She was old enough now to acknowledge her feelings of neglect, and at first used the Stewart's doting hospitality as a way of repaying herself some emotional currency. However, after the Fourth of July, the indoctrination truly began penetrating her psyche, and she slowly relinquished her apprehensions about the culture of Faith First.

When Steven and Jed turned eighteen, they both began romantically courting Maddy under the guise of "sibling bonding," as Madison was now practically a foster sister. Her presence was so ordinary, Martha and the girls set her a place at the dinner table every supper, and the whole family referred to the guest bedroom as "Maddy's study." Although she never actually spent the night, she was extended all the privileges of an adopted child. From the window of the downstairs bathroom at the Horn house, Bill and Jane could see the silhouettes inside the house across the street, but a fierce aversion to confrontation prevented them from even introducing themselves as neighbors. By winter's end, they had lost their daughter entirely.

In the Horn household, topics that were potentially upsetting or simply unpleasant were never mentioned, much less explored. But Madison's absence became so prevalent Bill decided to launch an investigation into Faith First. Through business contacts, he discovered that both the school and church were privately funded through donations, and had never been officially chartered or even recognized as having any affiliation with another religious institution.

He also learned that Gerry, on behalf of Faith First, had been named in a substantial civil law suit regarding the manipulation of a donor family and funds they had contributed. The plaintiff in the case was a woman named Cynthia Louis-Dumont—an heiress to the Dumont De Nemours family fortune— who had gifted Faith First 200,000 shares of her family's company stock from her trust. As the authorized party of his DBA, Gerry gradually sold the stock without restrictions and transferred the proceeds into a personal bank account he held jointly with Martha.

As Bill's investigation widened, he was put into contact with a man who knew the Dumont family and was familiar with their case. Bill learned that Cynthia, who was thirty-six at the time and had spent two years under the tutelage of Pastor G, was "abruptly transported" to a rural town in northern Maine to undergo a rigorous deprogramming. Shortly after her return, she founded The Center for Psychosocial Rehabilitation, for people recovering from "brainwashing" and other cult-like influences. Bill contacted the nearest chapter, which was in Troy, New York. When Cynthia caught word that Bill's daughter was directly involved with the same organization, she made a personal phone call to his office and offered him details about the man she had visited in Maine, who, she claimed, "gave her her life back."

Madison had developed a crush on Jed, but because Steven was his fraternal twin, they decided to keep their romantic inclinations quiet. Every night after the Stewarts went to bed, Maddy ran home and waited for his call. She would sit in her room with her hand gripping the receiver, and when it produced the slightest reverberation, she would whisk it up and whisper, "Is that you?" They often talked late into the night, and from these conversations they began to conceive a plan that would ultimately become the next five years of their lives.

One Friday evening in early May, five weeks before Maddy was due to graduate from Lenox High, she pedaled down to the corner store on Church Street to buy some penny candy for the movies. Jed and Steven had planned to borrow their parents' station wagon and take Maddy to the drive-in theater in North Adams. Maddy arrived at the store just before closing and parked her bike on the walk-up porch by the front façade. When she exited the store, clutching a heaping bag of sweets, her bike was gone. She looked around, puzzled, and began to survey the shadowy streets.

Suddenly her head was jerked backwards and a suffocating darkness blanketed her vision. The candy bag fell to the ground with a thud, and she heard Gobstoppers and Swedish Fish scatter across the pavement. A large, tight-knit winter hat was forced over her head and a dry rag was shoved into her mouth. She was lifted off her feet by four hands and her ankles were bound together by a thin, rubbery jump rope. She struggled mightily at first, but her screams were muffled. Quickly, her wrists were tied with a similar twine. As one of the hands grazed her exposed leg, she could tell from the brief touch that it was a woman. Neither of the assailants uttered a sound as they lowered her into their car. Maddy let out a continuously stifled shriek until she grew weary of breathing from her nose. The car ignition sputtered and stalled and she could hear the driver pump the gas pedal until the engine was revved up and ready. Through her mask, she detected the distinct aroma of pumpkin seeds mashed into the old plush upholstery.

CHAPTER 3

"Pumpkin seeds?" Smitty slides back in his seat, stretching his legs.

The Range Rover has been parked at a gas station just outside Wilmington, Delaware, but the engine is still running. Jay pauses the story.

"How long have we been sitting here?" They are both dazed and hungry.

"I have no idea, dude. I don't even know how we got here."

Axl is stretched out on his blankets, half asleep and breathing heavily. It is nighttime and the white neon street lights of the convenience store parking lot loom in the overhead like an artificial moon glow. Jay shuts off the engine and steps out to pump gas. After a few yawns, Smitty makes a break for the bathroom. Inside the store, they converge on the junk food aisle like moths mesmerized by a porch light. Bleary-eyed and smirking, they can barely look at each other without laughing. Jay grabs a package of beef jerky and heads to the register, trying to conceal the obviousness of two stoners on a road trip.

Back at the car, Smitty flings a package of ranch-flavored pumpkin seeds onto Jay's lap. He also hands him a large bottle of Gatorade.

"Continue," he proclaims, placing his palm in mid-air.

Jay snaps off a portion of his Slim Jim and hands it to Axl, who gobbles it up immediately.

"Where was I?" He starts the car and meanders back to the highway.

Smitty cracks open a package of Pepperidge Farm mint milanos.

"Pumpkin seeds," he replies, cookie crumbs spewing from his teeth.

Jay rips open his snack and dumps out a small portion into his hand, carefully lowering the savory seeds into his mouth.

"Right. Holy shit, I got the munchies."

"Fuckin' a right." Smitty takes an enormous gulp of Gatorade and Jay accelerates southward.

CHAPTER 4

About an hour into the ride, Maddy's mask was lifted off her head and the rag pulled from her mouth. A middle-aged woman with lank brown hair and uneven bangs leaned into the backseat. Maddy was unusually calm. The woman spoke for the first time, her voice gruff and raspy.

"We are not going to hurt you. My name is Ms. Lynne. And that's Raymond."

She pointed to the man driving the car and he flashed Maddy a quick glance through the rear-view mirror. Although Maddy was still in shock, she was too indignant to reply.

"The reason you are here is because we have been asked to help you."

Maddy turned her head and buried it into the seat. Ms. Lynne reached back and sternly tilted her chin so their eyes could meet.

"Listen to me. There is no need to be afraid. We are your friends." The concept of "friends" and "family" had been so malformed over the past year that the intrinsic meaning of the words held virtually no significance. She noticed that the floor was covered with candy bar wrappers, empty soda cans, an old Rubik's cube and stale pumpkin seeds. She had a fleeting thought of kicking her feet through the backseat window but restrained the impulse when she took another look at Raymond.

"Here, eat something."

Ms. Lynne opened the bag of penny candy Maddy had dropped in the street. Maddy refused without gesturing.

Another hour went by before anyone spoke again.

"Where are we *going*?" Maddy finally chirped.

"Liston County, Maine," Raymond answered in a no-nonsense tone.

Raymond intimidated Maddy. She had noticed that the motor oil fingerprints on her wrists and ankles matched the blackened hands that gripped the steering wheel. Periodically, he would scratch his neck and his ten-day scruff made a creepy bristling sound that was amplified by the quiet of the car. Ms. Lynne sat so stationary in the passenger seat, Maddy could not tell whether or not she had fallen asleep.

Raymond spoke up again. "It's a gott-damn shame a pretty girl like you ain't got no sense."

When Maddy heard this, she panicked. Until now, she assumed that the abduction was arranged by Pastor G, as something he called "a test of faith." From time to time, the children at the church would perform trust falls in the living room or become individually blindfolded and walk around the back-yard until they formed a circle holding hands. But no one affiliated with Faith First would take the Lord's name in vain.

When the car finally petered to a stop, Maddy could see nothing but the silhouettes of erect pine trees through the rear window. On the seat, the back of her head was pressed against an old sweatshirt that smelt like a fusion of cheddar cheese and stewed prunes. A crescent moon was tucked behind puffy night clouds and the air was cool and misty. Raymond got out first and opened the back door, springing Maddy's cramped feet forward. He untied the twine around her ankles, and as it loosened she felt a numbing sensation and a sharp tingle from the lack of blood flow. Ms. Lynne grabbed a raggedy blanket from the trunk and wrapped it around her as they stood her up. She reassured her, "Everyone here is your friend."

There was that word again.

§   §   §

The Horns sat at the dinner table eating Jane's reheated meatloaf. Neither of them spoke. When Bill was finished, he retired to the living room to watch the evening news. Jane cleared the table, washed the dishes, swept the floor and dusted the countertops. Then she went upstairs and closed the door to the bedroom. Bill fell asleep on the couch as the sounds of Johnny Carson and Ed McMahon droned on in the background. Four days had passed and still no word from Maine.

§   §   §

Maddy escaped shortly after arriving. The man performing the deprogramming was known only as Gaylen the Greek, minister of cognitive rebalancing. He was a lanky man with a wiry physique and a silvery ponytail that was tied into a frazzled knot. He spoke with a thinly veiled Mediterranean accent and always made stern eye contact when he addressed someone. In his backyard, a fully functional sweat lodge made from red clay protruded from the earth in the shape of a small tepee. Throughout the year, he hosted spiritual retreats on his property where people would meditate for sixteen hours a day, not speaking to each other until the weeklong session had concluded. The local community knew very little about Gaylen, as he was rarely spotted outside the boundaries of his own land. He did not have a phone, and the only car on his property was a 1983 Dodge Colt with expired Arkansas license plates. But from time to time, folk like Maddy were dropped off at his cabin, and while no other person knew the intricacies of his process, his word-of-mouth reputation for neutralizing the effects of brainwashing was unmatched.

Maddy abandoned the cabin before the deprogramming was complete. Gaylen had lost patience with her and went outside to prune a storm-ravaged spruce. He accounted for the possibility of her leaving, but decided it was best that she make her own decisions. Over the course of three days, Maddy had achieved some progress, but still had not quantified why she was brought there, who was behind it, and how the fundamentalist doctrine of Faith First had obstructed her ability to think freely. All she knew was that she just wanted to get back to Jed.

The soles of her frantic feet skimmed the unpaved road as she sprinted away, leaving tiny clouds of dirt behind each footstep. She was still dressed in Friday night's clothes, and as she ran her peach-colored blouse was darkened by sweat and dust. Her white Reebok tennis shoes were now covered in a thin, grimy film. Finally, she stopped and looked back. Nothing trailed her but her own shadow, which now hovered between the afternoon sunlight and the forest's outline. As she leaned over, she gasped for air and then exhaled with staccato repetition. When she stood up again, she noticed several burdocks were stuck to her hair and pants. Without further pause, she began running again until she came to an intersection three miles ahead.

In the distance, a Texaco logo protruded from a tall pole to the north, and she followed it to a filling station and repair garage. On the side of the road, she spotted a telephone booth where she immediately placed a collect call to the Stewarts' house.

§   §   §

Shortly before Bill was expected home from

work that afternoon, Jane walked out to the mailbox at the end of the driveway. As she was reaching for the mail, she heard the Stewarts' front door slam and saw Pastor G rush to his Caravan. She stopped short. As he backed out of his driveway, she turned her head, pretending not to notice him speed away.

§ § §

Maddy sat on a gravel curb until it was dark. Pastor G finally arrived at around nine PM. Maddy got in the van and they drove five hours back to Lenox without speaking. Gerry was content in pretending the whole incident never took place. When they got home, Maddy took a shower in the upstairs bathroom and Martha gave her one of her bathrobes. None of the children was permitted to visit with her or even ask where she had been. After the long shower, she went directly to the guest room and tucked herself under the covers. Her legs were sore from running, and her head ached from sadness and confusion. This was one time when the Stewarts chose not to offer a Bible lesson or prayer session and they simply left her alone. Maddy sandwiched her head between two pillows and cried silently until she fell asleep.

The next morning she trudged home

despondently. Bill was at work and Jane was grocery shopping. The house was locked but Maddy used the secret entrance through the garage. As she walked up to the door leading to the front hallway, she noticed her bike propped in its usual position in the corner. Her heart sunk. She stopped in the kitchen and found a trash bag under the sink and then went to her room to change her clothes. She put the outfit she had been wearing in the bag, tied the plastic drawstrings tightly and threw it in the back of her closet. Before she left, she stared at herself in the mirror until a soft, artificial smile emerged. She applied a thin layer of lipstick and eyeshadow and then went back down to the garage. Pushing the automatic opener, she snatched her bike and pedaled to the Stewart's house, deliberately leaving the garage door open.

Jed was waiting in the doorway when she returned. They embraced, and she whispered in his ear that she was sorry for leaving him.

CHAPTER 5

Jay loses his train of thought. For a few moments he stops talking and concentrates on the highway. The atmosphere grows still. Smitty notices that Jay's eyes are transfixed on a road sign ahead. As they pass the sign, Smitty reads it aloud slowly and inquisitively, and his excitement builds with each word.

"Cracker Barrel. Old Country Store and Restaurant! Open twenty-four hours!! Next right!"

Jay flicks on his turn signal and begins moving toward the exit.

"They got the killer biscuits and gravy." Smitty is partially hallucinating. "And we need to get you some coffee."

Jay mocks Smitty's *Fast Times At Ridgemont High* surfer intonation. "Caw-fee? Doood. All I need are some tasty waves, a cool buzz, and I'm fine..."

"Fuck off, Spicoli."

The parking lot at Cracker Barrel is almost completely empty as it is well past midnight. Jay shuts off the car.

"Are we in Virginia yet?"

"I hope so, I'm getting tired." Smitty begins to open his door but Jay stops him.

"Hold up. Aren't you forgetting something?" He reaches into the console and pulls out a blown glass one-hitter and packs it with pot.

"You're pretty fuckin' sharp tonight, Gordo."

"C'mon, you *have* to be stoned at Cracker Barrel. I think it's a legislative amendment once you cross the Mason Dixon."

"I'm pretty sure you're right about that." Smitty is grinning.

After two hits each, they both file into the restaurant. The woman who seats them is in her sixties and speaks in a heavy southern twang, leading them to believe that they *have* reached Virginia.

They both order coffee and the Old Timers' Breakfast: eggs, grits, buttermilk biscuits with Sawmill gravy, fried apples, hash brown casserole, and two strips of bacon.

"So, how long you been married now?" Jay broaches an awkward topic.

"Three years and four months," Smitty replies. "But she's still got that new wife smell."

Jay's follow-up thought tumbles into a boisterous giggle, and a middle-aged couple at an adjacent table, each with lit cigarettes

45

and full plates of food, fire off disapproving glances. Smitty has a pair of lightly tinted vintage Ray-Ban sunglasses perched on his head, which he lowers to cover his eyes. Jay resumes his inquisition.

"So, what's her name? Where's she from?"

Smitty stretches his neck back and rotates it from side to side.

"Lara," he says nonchalantly. "Cali girl. Her folks have giant dollars. Ever heard the name George Hogan?"

Jay quickly scans his memory lexicon then shakes his head.

"That was her grandfather. Dude was a big-time real estate developer in San Diego. He basically built up the footprint of the new city, and the family still holds all the leases." Jay salutes with a thumbs-up. "You must've had a hell of wedding."

"It was nice. We got fucked up. Wish you could have been there."

Carrying an outstretched tray, the waitress approaches the table. Jay and Smitty become instantly entrenched. Midway through their frenzy, Jay resumes his tale.

"So anyway..."

CHAPTER 6

Maddy did not attend the graduation ceremony at Lenox High. Instead she picked up her diploma from the main office shortly after the school year ended. Although she was still living at home, there was never any discussion of Maine, Faith First or her future plans. She had not applied to any colleges and dismissed the idea of finding a job in the local community. Bill and Jane had relinquished what little influence they had left and simply provided her with the necessary food and shelter.

One Sunday morning in late June, Maddy and Jed announced to the congregation that they were getting married. Everyone was shocked, including Pastor G, who delayed his sermon so he could speak to Jed in private. Steven took it especially hard. After hearing the news, he stormed out of the chapel and did not return. All the girls from school congratulated Maddy, but Martha stayed glued to her seat in the front pew, flexing a blank smile. As they were waiting for the pastor, they could hear his deep vocal tones reverberating through the plasterboard walls. Maddy felt the penetrating stares of the congregation, but through intense suppression, she had developed immunity from anxiety. Finally Gerry returned, but Jed was not with him. Without hesitation, he asked everyone to open their books and he went directly into his sermon. Maddy sat in the second row for the duration, and when it was over she went home.

Jed called later that night, as he always did.

"Hey, Madison!"

"Hey." Since returning from Maine, Maddy had become emotionally dependent on the Stewart family. And after everything that she had been through over the last year, she needed good news from Jed.

"Guess what?" He was so excited, he was nearly out of breath.

"What?" Maddy was tense.

"Father said that if we go to the Caribbean to do missionary work, when we get back he will pay for our wedding!"

"What? Really?"

This was not what she had expected. It was a culmination of her prepubescent ambitions to escape from the world she knew and separate herself from her past.

When Maddy packed her suitcase, she took no personal artifacts or books; just clothes, shoes and makeup. Then she pulled out the plastic bag she had hidden in her closet three months earlier. She opened it and placed her Lenox High: Class of 1989 senior yearbook amongst the dirty garments. After her parents were asleep, she snuck outside and hid the bag in the loft above the garage. She set up a small cot in the corner and found an old Afghan crocheted by her grandmother, which she used as a blanket. Maddy would never spend another night in her old bedroom.

Over the next eighteen months, Maddy and Jed became inseparable. The Caribbean missionary program was started by an organization called Bible Wise, based in eastern Maryland. All seven missionaries traveled through the Caribbean together on a rickety, chartered boat. They spent three months building churches and seeding "the message" throughout townships in Jamaica, Barbados, Haiti, the Dominican Republic and Grenada. One night while in Haiti, Jed snuck into Maddy's tent and woke her. In his hand he held a beaded ring that was handcrafted by a local woman. He slipped it on her finger and began kissing her softly. Two nights later, they had sex for the first time. Maddy wore that ring until the day they were married, when it was replaced by a modest diamond.

A month before the program was scheduled to end, a few members of the group finally exposed Maddy and Jed for having premarital sex. Discreetly, they were asked to leave. From the missionary boarding house, it was a three-hour taxi ride to Point Salines International airport. Using some of the money they had saved, they each purchased one-way tickets to Baltimore. With the exception of Steven, who was living and working at a Christian sports camp in West Virginia, the entire Faith First family met them in Maryland. True to his word, Pastor G paid for their wedding, which was held at the Bible Wise congregation on the outskirts of Salisbury. Bill and Jane Horn were not invited.

§ § §

Married life began in student housing at New York University. Much to the chagrin of his father, Jed decided he wanted to de-emphasize his religious devotion, and instead harness his intellectual prowess as a finance student. Maddy dutifully supported the decision and began looking for secretarial jobs in Manhattan. Eventually, she found work as a paralegal at Dobson & Verlander, a prestigious midtown law firm. With Jed engrossed in his studies, they barely found time for each other. This routine lasted for nearly two years.

Jed was disowned by his family when he enrolled at NYU. Pastor G always said, "Secular society is no place for a good Christian," and he stuck to this ideology from the moment Jed refused to consider Jerry Falwell's Liberty University. Consequently, neither Jed nor Maddy maintained any contact with their families. They were each just twenty years old.

CHAPTER 7

In the fall of 1993, Jed began an internship in the corporate finance division at Goldman Sachs. To pay for his tuition, fees and living expenses, Maddy worked seventy hours a week. They no longer attended Sunday services at the Latter Day Worship Center, and neither engaged in any social activities or friendships. Yet inside their small studio apartment, a silent rift wedged itself between them, until it became evident that their relationship was deteriorating.

Dobson & Verlander began working on a heady prospectus for a private equity firm. After a series of meetings, their client, Ron Petersen, took a particular liking to Maddy's appearance and demeanor. He offered her a position as a sales assistant at the fund and he doubled her annual salary. Maddy signed on without hesitation.

At Petersen Capital Management, Maddy met Rachel Rothstein, a trader and research analyst. At twenty-five, Rachel was an emerging prodigy on Wall Street. She had graduated top of her class at Stanford University and then gotten her MBA through an accelerated program at UC Berkeley's Haas School of Business. Maddy had never admired a woman before she met Rachel. They bonded instantly. Forever branded as an "intellectual jock," Rachel was drawn to Maddy's fun-loving, hyper-feminine innocence, and Maddy appreciated Rachel's straight-talk tough-love regarding her sheltered zeitgeist.

After work one evening, they went out for a drink and Maddy, who had never even sipped an alcoholic beverage, guzzled three Cosmopolitans and spent the rest of the evening hugging porcelain in the bathroom at the Plaza. Later that night she took a cab home, and when Jed returned from the office she broke the news that she was drunk and had been working at a hedge fund for nearly two months. Uncharacteristically, Jed lost his composure, and for the first time ever they raised their voices and argued.

Through Rachel, Maddy gained an intimate knowledge of the secular world. Rachel was a "Christmas tree Jew" from Bay Shore, who had spent six academic years in northern California and blended distinct mannerisms from each region. (A New York burrito was "hella ow-ful," but a slice from Grimaldi's in Brooklyn was "super bomb.")

Together they honed a taste for expensive lunches and boutique shopping on Fifth Avenue. Maddy quickly abandoned her prudent ways. She made weekly appointments to get her hair trimmed and highlighted. She always had a fresh manicure and pedicure and she developed an obsession for high-end makeup. At first, she tried coaxing Jed into a more material existence: French restaurants and Broadway shows on a Saturday night; but he was far too austere and devoted to his coursework to join Maddy in such frivolity.

In January of 1994, Maddy decided she no longer wanted to live on the Lower East Side. Rachel's friend Mira was a leasing agent, and found them a large, one-bedroom on 77th Street off Amsterdam Avenue. Jed was vehemently opposed to moving but Maddy insisted, citing that she was the one supporting him. Jed grew bitter with resentment and they barely spoke to one another. The extra space in their Upper West Side flat became symbolic of how they had grown apart since the days of building lean-tos and sleeping in pitch tents in the Caribbean.

The workday at Petersen Capital grew progressively demanding, and Maddy started spending a few nights a week at Rachel's place. Indeed, it was logistically closer to the office, but she did it more as an excuse to drift from her husband. She began to see him as a man who was brutishly unsophisticated and so book-sharp he was dull. As a result, they stopped having sex and when they did sleep in the same bed, the feeling of reluctance slept between them.

One Monday, before the opening bell on the New York Stock Exchange, Madison dialed her home in Lenox to see if the number had changed. Jane answered in her usual timid voice.

"Hullo?"

Earlier that morning, while staring at an Old Spice ad on the subway, Maddy had decided to reach out to her parents. For weeks she had battled the feelings of loneliness and nostalgia, but finally she relented. So much had happened since she last spoke with her family.

"Mom?"

When Mrs. Horn heard her daughter's voice, she burst into a restrained weep. Maddy heard the quiet sniffling and her throat thickened, but she managed to find the words to invite her parents to dinner. With a quivering voice, Jane agreed.

They met at an Italian restaurant in Greenwich, Connecticut, a less overwhelming setting for Bill and Jane, who had never been to New York City. Bill was defiant about expressing pity or contrition and maintained a gruff demeanor throughout the evening. Maddy had inherited his pride and stubbornness. During dinner, Jane was typically muted, yet inwardly pleased to finally reunite with her estranged daughter. Madison explained that because of her tenuous relationship with Jed, she was uncomfortable going home, not wanting to run into her in-laws. Bill sat expressionless, but Jane's jaw dropped. Then she explained about her marriage. The Horns just nodded stiffly without offering any emotion or words. After dinner, they exchanged awkward, affectionless parting salutations and Maddy promised that she would call from time to time. The next time she spoke to her parents, she was divorced.

§   §   §

Maddy and Rachel were sent on a business trip to Los Angeles during the spring of 1995. It was also Jed's graduation week at NYU. Hassan Raji, a managing director at Goldman Sachs, was the only person who attended the commencement dinner and ceremony on behalf of Jed.

To help fill the void of a defunct marriage, Maddy had cultivated a cover-to-cover addiction for glamour magazines and celebrity tabloids. In between meetings in Pasadena and beach excursions in Venice, she used the rest of her time to visit "hot spots" she had read about. Although Rachel was underwhelmed by the paparazzi culture, she found a spectator's enjoyment in Maddy's childlike enthusiasm.

The night before they returned to New York, Petersen Capital acquired a mid-sized insurance company through a leveraged buyout. Their partner in the deal was an independent venture capitalist by the name of Julian Bixby. The two parties involved went out for dinner and drinks at Sky Bar on Sunset Boulevard. Maddy, who not had not yet really cultivated a taste for alcohol, drank two glasses of white wine and more dirty vodka martinis than she could remember. Toward the end of the night she was slumped in a pile on a plush sofa overlooking the sprawling city. Her hair was disheveled and her dark eye shadow was smeared under her eyelids. Julian Bixby approached with two glasses of champagne, and when Maddy looked up she was instantly smitten.

Mr. Bixby was a former standout in the Australian Rugby League. He was six-foot-four, two-hundred-sixty-five pounds, and when he spoke his cheery Aussie drawl was both captivating and intimidating. He'd retired from "football" in the late eighties and used his notoriety to start a venture capital business in Sydney. Years later he moved to San Francisco and used his liquidity to devour opportunities in the U.S. markets. Ron Petersen had estimated Bixby's net worth at somewhere between ten and thirty million, and viewed the completion of their first deal as "a direct pipeline to limitless possibility." Prior to the trip, Maddy was given the responsibility of investigating Mr. Bixby and his complex enterprises. Her report was an internal template used to gauge the merits of their potential partnership. Maddy knew various details about Julian and his company but had never met the man himself.

"Don't tell me you're too ti'ed for moor champine," he smirked, leaning down and extending a bubbly crystal glass.

Maddy sat up in her seat and tucked a wisp of hair behind her ear. Her wedding ring was tucked away inside the suitcase in her room at the Wyndham Bel Age. She had removed it before the plane landed at LAX.

"I was just resting," she said, blushing. The room was spinning and she was dizzy.

"Oh, good, 'ere ya go then." Julian handed her the glass and proposed a toast. "To fewcha endeavahs."

"To future endeavors." Maddy clinked

his glass and took a tiny sip. After that, she blacked out.

§   §   §

The next morning she woke up with a vicious hangover. Rachel was hovering in the entranceway and had taken the liberty of packing Maddy's bags, but Maddy would not get out of bed.

"The car service is waiting downstairs. You have to get up, Madison. We're going to miss the flight."

Maddy rolled over and groaned, "Jesus is merciful. Jesus is merciful."

Rachel was agitated. "Oh, for God's sake, would you stop this!" She walked over to the bed and tried pulling the covers away from her head. Maddy shrieked.

"No! I have to let God punish me. I am a bad wife. I am a terrible person."

Maddy sounded so self-pitying Rachel was now amused.

"You're just hung over. You never drank too much and felt sick the next day?"

"I am sick because God is punishing me. But Jesus is merciful."

On the desk across from the bed, Rachel found a notepad and a pen. She jotted some information down and tore the sheet from the pad, placing it on Maddy's suitcase. Without saying anything else, she left the room. When Maddy heard the door slam, she sat up in bed. She was wearing only a bra. When she realized that Rachel had left, she slumped back under the sheets and fell asleep. It was late afternoon when she finally got up. Her head ached and her stomach was knotted. She took a long shower and got dressed. As she was leaving the room, she found Rachel's note.

> *Sorry I couldn't wait. See you in New York.*
> *LAX terminal 4. American Airlines flight 467 to JFK. Change your ticket at the gate or fly stand-by. Remember to call your husband and let him know you'll be late!*
> *~RR*
> *P.S. Jesus is merciful.*

When Maddy read this, a half smile crept onto her lips. She picked up her bags and folded the note inside her Louis Vuitton bag. Then she rode the elevator down to the lobby. As she approached the concierge she heard a familiar voice coming from the hotel bar.

"I ordered you an appetizer. I thought you might need to eat something."

Maddy wheeled around and saw Rachel sitting by a fireplace sipping cabernet. It was early evening and the California sun was rich and radiant as it poured into the room.

Rachel had decided not to fly back to New York and instead had reserved a penthouse suite in the same hotel. She figured "girls night out" on the Sunset Strip would be a nice remedy for Maddy's hangover. Maddy was so elated she forgot to call Jed and reschedule their celebratory dinner.

By nightfall, Maddy and Rachel had finished hors d'oeuvres and moved their bags into the suite on the top floor. Rachel had been waiting for the right moment to divulge a secret.

"There's somebody who would like to see you tonight."

Maddy's eyes lit up. "Julian?"

Rachel nodded.

"He stopped by the hotel earlier. I told him you were out shopping. I have the number where he's staying."

Conflict set in as Maddy unconsciously massaged her empty ring finger. After a long deliberation, she resolved to forego his dinner invitation and meet for drinks later in the evening. This time she wore her wedding ring.

Only a few blocks east from the Wyndham Bel Age, Sky Bar was the setting once again. Before Julian arrived in the terrace lounge, Maddy spent nearly fifteen minutes primping in the ladies room.

§   §   §

Back in New York, Jed sat by the kitchen table in a plain wool suit, peering out the window as yellow cabs passed without stopping. Eventually he shifted to the couch, flipped on the television and fell asleep in his clothes.

§   §   §

Rachel entertained Julian at the bar until Maddy emerged. A virgin cocktail was waiting, and during their initial interaction she sipped it as if it were a Cosmo. Within the first minute, Julian observed the ring on Maddy's finger that had not been there the night before. He took notice without drawing attention to his acknowledgment, and made a gentlemanly amendment to his preconceived plan. After thirty minutes, he motioned to the exit and whispered something in Maddy's ear. Rachel accompanied them to the elevator and down to the street where the valet was waiting with Julian's silver Aston Martin DB 7 convertible. His California vanity license plate read HATE ME. Maddy slipped into the passenger seat and Rachel shimmied into the back. Julian promised a view of the city and a breeze from the mountains. As he drove out onto Sunset Boulevard, he twisted the stereo knob up until AC/DC's "For Those About to Rock" overtook the ambiance. Maddy's hair fluttered in the dry night air, and the engine of the DB 7 gently purred as the velocity increased. He made a right on Laurel Canyon Boulevard and headed north to the intersection of Mulholland Drive. Pausing at the stoplight, he cocked his neck to the side so his long bangs could cascade.

"Ladies, 'old on to yoah hats," he cautioned, before tearing down the hilly road.

Rachel had to turn her head, nearly laughing through her nose, but Maddy was enamored. When they reached the turnoff for Dante's Peak, Julian simultaneously killed the music and headlights. The expansive City of Angels sparkled below. From underneath his seat, he pulled out a bottle of Dom Perignon and two champagne glasses, pouring each lady a generous taste. Rachel politely sipped from her glass, but it was obvious now that her presence had not been anticipated.

§   §   §

When Maddy returned to the Upper West Side, she noticed Jed had moved his suits and ties into the hall closet. In the starchy world of a banking analyst, this was the first sign he was giving up on his marriage. It was late evening when Maddy walked into the apartment. She plopped her bags down by the coat-rack and flipped on the hall lights. On the end table next to the couch, she spotted Jed's New York University diploma. It was wrapped in a clear, laminated folder next to a caved-in Juicy Juice box under the lamp. Jed was not home. A momentary wave of nostalgia overtook Maddy as she stood in the entranceway. The sight of his diploma and her absence from the ceremony brought back memories of high school—how she had missed her own graduation to spend the afternoon with Jed—and how such feelings had all but completely faded. She heard Julian's debonair tenor echoing in her ears and she could still taste expensive champagne on the back of her tongue. The contrast to her husband's deflated juice box was noteworthy.

It took awhile for them to entertain the prospects of a legal separation, as both Madison and Jed came from places where most things were never discussed. By the time he filed for divorce in 1996, it had been over a year since they'd had sex.

Maddy got into the habit of coming in late to work and working late. One night, at around eight PM in the east, she decided to call Julian at his office in San Francisco. During their conversation, she happened to mention how "exhausting" it was to go through a divorce. Julian promptly invited her to his farmhouse in Napa Valley for a weekend so she could "relax" and "clear her mind." Maddy accepted the invitation and told Jed she was going on another business trip. Before she left, she made an appointment for a bikini wax.

When she landed in San Francisco on a Friday night, Julian was waiting in a black Land Rover Defender. In the backseat he had two shopping bags from Neiman Marcus. Not knowing her size, he had bought three pairs of tie-side thongs, three pairs of tulle hipster knickers and three black corsets.

Maddy resisted sleeping with him on the first night, but after dinner at the French Laundry and a moonlit wine picnic at a vineyard, she surrendered herself on night number two. The sex was exhilarating, as Maddy was tantalized both by Julian's outback charm and her own guilt. The greater part of Sunday was spent under the covers making love repeatedly until Maddy had to catch her flight back to New York. Julian promised next time he would come to visit her.

Throughout the divorce proceedings, Maddy remained contritely amicable. She let Jed keep the apartment and moved her now abundant material possessions into a storage unit on 11th Avenue. For two months she slept on Rachel's couch and continued working at the hedge fund. But, from the time she left San Francisco, all she could think about was Julian Bixby.

CHAPTER 8

Thirty minutes northwest of Virginia Beach, Jay and Smitty make camp at the Kingsmill Resort and Spa. Axl sprints around the parking lot, fetching his favorite chewed up teddy bear, and Smitty feeds him some leftover bacon. After unpacking, they trudge inside to check in. Axl waits in the car. While escorting them to their room, the concierge informs Jay that pets are not permitted inside the hotel. Exhausted from their seven-hour drive, they brainstorm at the mini-bar over two scotches. From his suitcase, Smitty pulls out a small stash of Demerol. Jay chuckles and they chase painkillers with single malts. Before the buzz intensifies, Jay empties out his golf clubs in order to smuggle Axl inside the elongated sack. Smitty volunteers to act as a decoy, sparking inconsequential conversation with the front desk, until Jay emerges wrestling a misshapen golf bag with three clubs protruding from the side. Smitty's leer almost gives them away, but he manages to end his chat in time to join Jay and Axl at the elevator.

In the bathroom of the two-room suite, Jay sets up a water dish and snack tray for Axl, who now seems equally exhausted.

"Fuck an early tee time tomorrow, I'm sleepin' in." Smitty's mouth is full of toothpaste.

"Did you put the thing on the door?"

Demerol has diminished the coherency of their dialogue.

After brushing his teeth, Jay gives Axl a goodnight ear rub. Then he and Smitty share a brief, machismo half-hug.

"It's good to see you again, Gordy. This is gonna be a great fucking trip."

Jay stays in the bathroom with the dog, petting him gently until he is sedate.

At 5:45 AM he is awoken suddenly by the sound of Axl's loud, allegro woofs. His head is puffy from an inebriated fatigue, yet he catapults out of bed with the quickness of a fire chief responding to his CB. Wearing only boxer shorts, he races to the other side of the room where he finds his dog howling at the blue glow of Smitty's television. On screen, a graphic pornography scene has incited Axl's fury and his barks are sharp and persistent. Smitty is out cold and the TV remote is ensconced amidst the ruffled duvet. In a panic, Jay leaps toward the set and scrambles in the dark for the power button but he cannot find it. Smitty senses the commotion and rolls over. A symphony of expletive moaning grows louder and louder, and Jay realizes that the TV volume is increasing. Axl calms down but the visceral porno soundtrack is blaring at top volume. Realizing that Smitty is lying on the remote, Jay pounces on his bed and begins rummaging through the blankets. On impact, Smitty wakes up startled and disoriented. He feels Jay's hand fishing furiously near his genitals.

"Whoa! The fuck are you doing?!"

Jay finds the remote and presses the power button. Smitty flips on his bedside lamp. Both are groggy and agitated, but after a few minutes it becomes humorous.

"Jesus Christ. You give this fuckin' guy a little scotch and a painkiller and he turns into Boy George. This isn't *Brokeback Mountain*, asshole."

Jay returns serve and the insults fly back and forth.

"You're a real sick fuck ordering porn with another guy in the room."

"You were in my bed—*my bed*, groping for my *unit*!"

"You didn't hear Axl barking?"

"Not cool, bro. Not cool."

Jay shakes his head and Smitty yawns.

"How old are we? It's like we never left Chapman."

"Yeah, and you're Charlie McGurdy, you fuckin' perv!"

Both burst out laughing as they reminisce about MHA's notorious masturbator.

"Charlie McGurdy!" Smitty hasn't heard that name in fifteen years.

"We laugh, but that fuckin' prick-puller is probably some dotcom tycoon."

"They're gonna kick us out of here. You know that, right?"

"Fuck it. I'll go now. The hell with golf and fuck my brother-in-law. "

"I'm going to bed. Keep that TV off, Pee-Wee Herman."

Daybreak softens the pigmented purple horizon. Jay coaxes Axl into the bathroom, slides back into bed and drifts into a deep slumber.

CHAPTER 9

In the winter of 1998, Jay returned from a vacation in Mexico determined to open an upscale bistro in his hometown. With a bachelor's degree in management from Cornell and nearly a decade of industry experience, he understood the intricacies of this venture. At the time, U.S. equity markets were mid-surge in a historic run. Conversely, real estate was stagnant. Although per capita income in Lenox is significantly higher than America's median, local businesses still rely heavily on the discretionary spending habits of tourists.

Many people close to Jay advised against opening a restaurant downtown until the second home market regained its bullish impetus. But Jay placed a bet against the trend. He purchased a commercial building just off Main Street and began renovations in early 1999. Working closely with contractors and architects, he designed a modern, French-inspired bistro with a cozy yet elegant dining area and a full service bar in the adjacent room. The whole project took nearly fourteen months to complete. Jay was leveraged to the max, and was now dependent on food and liquor sales. Yet since the furniture and wall fixtures had not arrived and a staff had not been hired, the opening was at least a month away. At this point the naysayers came out in full force, but Jay just kept on working. He spent twenty hours a day at the restaurant, coordinating everything from employee interviews to the table layouts, and he was adamant about the aesthetics. In the dining area, the synergy of candlelight and white linen created a warm golden glow that enunciated the décor. Behind the bar, a spotless mirror traced the wall's perimeter, and each bottle of Glenrothes Scotch, Louis XIII cognac, and Jay's personal collection of small-batch bourbons reflected with enticing effervescence. Finally his handmade sign arrived and he proudly hung it on a polished chrome pole by the sidewalk. It was a chic, silver engraving, with simple blue letters that spelled MAISON, a French word meaning home.

Three nights before the open, everything had fallen into place. Even the linen had arrived on time. The kitchen was equipped, the bar was stocked, and a photo gallery of black and white framed portraits hung throughout the restaurant. Jay invited Boca

Josh, a college friend he had known since grade school, down to help him revel in his glory. Josh acquired the handle "Boca" during spring break of their sophomore year at Cornell. One afternoon in early March, he left Ithaca on a Florida-bound Greyhound bus. Two weeks later, Jay and his suitemates received an anonymous postcard from Boca Raton. Josh did not return to college until the following fall.

Boca and Jay sat around an empty bar and drank bottle after bottle of Château Petrus. By the end of the night, Boca straddled his stool with a limp, and Jay was sprawled out on the glossy hardwood floors singing Mötley Crüe's "Home Sweet Home." After ten years, his ambition was finally a reality and Jay Gordon was now a restaurateur.

CHAPTER 10

Maddy quit her job and moved to San Francisco in 1999. Julian was merging one of his Australian protégé VC companies, and split his time between Sydney and California. Maddy had been fully integrated as his "girlfriend" and she enjoyed the lavish privileges associated with such a designation. Most days she slept in, ordered delivery from the Biltmore Hotel and drove his black Defender around the hilly city until she grew bored. She knew no one and made no attempt to meet anyone. Instead, she immersed herself in daytime soaps, Meg Ryan movies and boutique shopping. Twice a month, Julian would return and they would sojourn at his Napa Valley cabin for the weekend. This routine lasted nearly four months. After his business in Sydney was complete, Julian bought Maddy a $375,000 Harry Winston engagement ring and left it on the breakfast bar with a note his assistant had typed. It read:

```
I remember the way your eyes looked
the night I met you. May there
be many more memories between us.
Meet me for lunch at Luna Park
```

74

today. I would be honored if you
would consider being my wife.
-J.W.B.

Maddy was awed by the size of the diamond. But the fit was wrong, so when she
went to meet Julian for lunch, she goofishly
wore it on her pinky. Julian was an hour late.
When he arrived, he saw his eight carats dangling from her little finger and was furious.
He bellowed, "You look like a trashy who'ah,"
and Maddy just sat there and smiled. Naturally she was embarrassed, but to her a public berating felt something like raindrops on
a duck's back. She put the ring in the box
and tucked it away in one of her new purses.
Julian did not stay to eat.

Their engagement was officially consum-
mated later that evening when he apologized
for his outburst, claiming he was annoyed by
Ron Petersen, her old boss. Afterwards, they
talked about the wedding. Julian suggested
Maui, Sydney, or Napa Valley, but Maddy
had a different idea: Lenox.

CHAPTER 11

Smitty awakes in the hotel room, and without getting up flips on ESPN. SportsCenter is no longer airing, an indication that it is well past noon. He hops out of bed and pulls open the drapes. A midday haze floods the room. Axl notices the light and rattles his collar as he trots out to greet him. At the other end of the room, Jay is still sound asleep. After a shower and shave, Smitty puts up a pot of coffee to create the aroma of morning. Jay finally stirs and painstakingly sits up in bed. It is 1:15 PM.

"Jeeeesuuuus." He lets out a long, silent yawn until his jowls deflate. "Let's get some food."

Over lunch in the dining area downstairs, Jay continues unspooling his saga while Axl waits patiently in the room. During checkout, he is temporarily stuffed back into the golf bag and transported to the Range Rover. Smitty decides to forgo a golf rendezvous with his brother-in-law. It is late afternoon by the time they are back on the highway and dark rain clouds begin forming on the southern horizon. Hilton Head Island, South Carolina, is their next destination, but with a storm looming, another seven-hour drive seems unlikely at this hour of the day. Smitty rolls a thin, tight joint to pass the time and Jay cues up a quintessential playlist of eighties head-banger ballads.

As the spliff smoke ripples throughout the car and the triumphant finale of Damn Yankees' "High Enough" evaporates, Smitty poses a question:

"What ever happed to that girl you were seeing from UMass-Amherst?"

Jay smiles and shakes his head, pitter-puffing on the roach clutched between his thumb and index finger.

"We broke up a few months before I opened Maison. It got to the point with Kiki where I had to either put a ring on her finger or let her go. I never saw us getting married so... Shit, I haven't spoken with her in six, seven years. You remember my friend Boca Josh?"

Smitty squints his eyes in recollection. "Vaguely."

"Boca's wife knows Kiki's family by coincidence. Last time I heard, she was married to some sales executive, living in Florida and sunning herself at the country club all day."

Smitty twists his mouth as if say, "Yikes."

"Well, whatever dude. If she's happy… But after close to five years of almost-marriage I know as well as anybody that she ain't easy to please."

Smitty takes the roach. "C'mon. That's no aberration, Jay. If pleasing women were easy…"

Jay smiles introspectively. "Trust me, I know! But you haven't even heard *my* whole story yet."

CHAPTER 12

One decade, one husband, one divorce and two engagements spanned the time between when Maddy left Massachusetts and returned. But she always clung to the concept of a storybook wedding in her hometown, with her proud parents beaming and applauding in the front row. In the months that preceded the ceremony, Julian refused to discuss any preparations. On one occasion he flatly told Madison that his only responsibility was to write the checks and say "I do." Maddy, who had plenty of time to plan, eventually chose Wheatleigh as their nondenominational chapel. Before calling her parents to break the news, she wrote down what she would say and then rehearsed her joyful confession in the mirror until she was comfortable with her delivery. But when her father answered, her voice grew quivery and she forgot her lines.

"Daddy?"

A long pause ensued. "Where are you?"

"Is Mom there?" Another pause.

Bill slid the receiver away from his mouth. "Jane. Your daughter's on the phone."

Maddy's heart rate picked up pace. "Wait, Dad. Stay on the phone for just a minute."

79

While she was waiting for Jane, she quickly glanced at her notes but ultimately decided to ad lib. Her parents' reaction was more temperate than she had hoped for, although they each voiced their appreciation for not having to travel to the ceremony. She explained that all the arrangements—financially and otherwise—were taken care of, and all they had to do was to invite Johnny, Jackie and Jerry, and show up in time for vows. They agreed, but expressed apprehension about inviting her brothers. Jerry was secretly living at a pristine drug-rehab facility in Connecticut. John and Jack were dispersed throughout the country and could not attend. Nevertheless, Maddy was satisfied.

Julian's work demanded limitless time and energy, and his temper was often as volatile as his business ventures. Although he possessed the material pedigree of a debonair romantic, his sensibility was that of a surly hermit. And despite his savvy in the private equity world, he was widely disliked by both competitors and associates. The concept of matrimony was somewhat of a formality to him, a necessary security in a portfolio of career accomplishments.

The oafish charm he initially exuded while courting Maddy never reappeared once she committed herself to him. For Madison, the wedding, in essence, became more of a break in the monotony than a fortification of a commitment. Fittingly, he decided to pack his work schedule until the night before vows were exchanged. Maddy traveled home a week prior to visit with her family and supervise the production. She also enjoyed six nights alone in the Aviary suite at the Wheatleigh Hotel.

Returning to Lenox harkened a barrage of displaced memories and confusing emotions. It was the first time she had been home since leaving in a T-top TransAm when she was eighteen. Her old bedroom had been transformed into a tidy guest room with flowery wallpaper and matching potpourri baskets, but its sterile starkness left the impression that it was never used. During dinner, Maddy focused on her pot roast, carefully cutting it as the tinkering of silverware was the only conversation at the table. Afterwards, she slipped into the hallway bathroom to sneak a peak at the Stewarts' house across the street. Both the house and the adjacent complex were painted differently and the Faith First signs were gone. The grass in the front yard was long and untended and a bed of weeds grew fervently in the garden Martha used to obsessively blanket in pesticides. She took a moment to process everything before returning to the table for Entenmann's carrot cake and decaf.

Julian arrived the night before the wedding. He declined an invitation to meet her family for dinner, citing "terrible jet lag." So they ordered room service and built a robust fire.

The next morning, Maddy awoke at nine AM to meet Rachel, who was driving up from New York City in a rental car. Aside from putting on her vintage Valentino gown and Manolo Blahnik shoes, seeing Rachel was the one thing she was excited about. They met at Church Street Café in downtown Lenox and sat outdoors sipping cappuccinos in the early summer sun. It was Rachel's first visit to the Berkshires and she was enamored by the lush countryside and tidy architecture.

In public, Maddy had a custom of always wearing oversized Chanel sunglasses. As glamour magazines replaced the King James Bible, celebrity style became her primary religion, and although she was a child of rural roots, she now considered herself "completely cosmopolitan."

The Bixbys rented the entire Wheatleigh Hotel for the weekend. Even the vacant rooms were paid for. Ironically, vacancies outnumbered guests. The ceremony itself was quick and quaint, and Julian's vows were surpris-

ingly well-conceived given his lack of preparation. Bill and Jane sat in the front row
smiling—just as Maddy had imagined—and
Jerry had managed to spring free from rehab
and sneak into the ceremony shortly before it
commenced. Although he was disheveled and
improperly dressed, the sight of her youngest
brother brought tears to her eyes.

A few of Julian's former rugby teammates
flew in from Australia and got sufficiently
smashed before entering the wedding hall.
Afterwards, everyone adjourned to the parlor
for dinner and drinks. It was an odd reception as the crowd was awkwardly congenial
until appropriate alcohol levels were achieved.
After the main course, Bill and Jane walked
to the bridal table, handed Maddy an envelope, shook Julian's hand and excused themselves. This created an opportunity for the
elderly guests, mostly Maddy's extended family, to exit as well. A few hours later, Maddy
insisted on shifting the wedding party into
town. With a polished, four-drink charisma,
she began asking employees at Wheatleigh
if they could recommend a bar setting that
might be appropriate. One of the porters was
an intern from France, studying American
fine food service. His older brother was a sous
chef at the bistro Maison.

Maddy was delighted by the name and

she phoned over to gauge the capacity restrictions. She spoke to the hostess, who got clearance from the owner. The only stipulation was that the whole party needed to be out of the bar five minutes prior to closing. Having only been open for a week, the strict enforcement of liquor laws was imperative.

CHAPTER 13

It was a Saturday night in early June. Jay sat in his office at Maison staring at a spreadsheet and pondering sales numbers. Although it had only been a week, lunch and dinner receipts were already exceeding expectations. A whispering within the culinary community was building, and college kids home on summer break kept the bar buzzing through last call. He gazed out the window and noticed that a series of Lincoln Town Cars had just pulled into the parking lot. After a few data comparisons, he left his office to greet the wedding party. Hugh, a youthfully handsome man for forty-five, was the lone bartender on duty. Dressed in a crisp, black button-up, his salt 'n' pepper hair was gently sculpted and a boyish smile gave him the look of someone fifteen years younger. Hugh and Jay shared a long history in the service industry. When Jay first segued from server to bartender, he trained as Hugh's barback and they had remained friends over the years. Before he even developed the floor plan for Maison, Jay appointed Hugh his bar manager.

Settling into the front corner of the bar, Jay carefully took note of the well-dressed revelers as they filed in. Arriving fashionably late, Madison glided through the open doors with the grace of Ingrid Bergman at an Oscar party. She was still wearing her Valentino gown, and her enormous Graff canary diamond studded earrings sparkled in the mirrors behind the bar.

Jay was mesmerized. Slowly, the commotion in the room faded and his breathing grew sluggish, as if each inhale was a moment he was unconsciously savoring. His vision was transfixed, which left his observations more wistful than subtle. Maddy had a contagious smile, and every so often he noticed her exhale a puff of air upwards so her perfectly styled bangs would flutter in place. After what felt like an hour, he unlocked his eyes and blinked them repeatedly, finally turning his head toward Hugh. He decided he needed a drink. Hugh bounded agilely from end to end, mixing martinis and pouring champagne in friendly, frantic pace. Ever so discreetly, Jay slipped back into his office for a glass of Patron Silver.

There was something bitterly surrealistic

about encountering a woman who transfixes your vision and shortens your breath on the night of her wedding to someone else. Jay wrestled with this thought as he sipped his tequila.

Julian and his rugby buddies were midway through an epic binge. From inside his office, Jay could hear them singing fight songs and pounding Jagermeister shots with whiskey and beer chasers. Maddy sat at a corner table in the back, delicately sipping a Cosmo. She chatted with guests and toasted strangers, and if it were not for the wedding garb, it would appear that the bride and groom did not even know each other. Rachel tried to arrange a dance between the newlyweds, but Julian changed the subject quickly by insisting she take a shot with "the boys."

With a tinge of apprehension, Jay stepped out from his office and walked directly up to Maddy. Since she was sitting, he hoped she would notice him before he approached, but she did not look in his direction until he was hovering in her presence.

"And you must be the lovely bride." Jay sounded confident but internally he questioned his opening statement.

"Madison Bixby." She extended her hand and her wedding ring glistened in the light. It was the first time she had used Julian's surname, and Jay sensed some hesitation in the fluidity of her introduction.

"Jay Gordon." He shook her hand slowly. "Well, congratulations. Welcome. If there is anything you need, please do not hesitate." Jay was warming up and grew more comfortable with each word.

"This is your place?" Maddy played coy.

"Yeah. She's just a baby but we're expecting great things." He gave her a convincing wink.

"I love the name. What does it mean?"

"Home," Jay replied. "And it's just like home except you can't raid the fridge when you're drunk." A proverbial lead balloon plummeted with a thud. Julian and company broke into song again, which averted an awkward pause.

"Well, it was nice meeting you, congratulations again." Jay made his escape quickly, assuming that Madison was unimpressed.

"Not exactly a match made in heaven," he muttered to Hugh as he approached the bar. Hugh nodded toward Julian, who was head-butting one of his friends. Jay chuckled softly and looked back at Maddy, who was staring at her husband with a look of incredulity.

"One of the Australian guys ordered a bunch of pizzas from Domino's in Pittsfield."

"Fuck, Hugh!" This was a recurring joke

that never got old to Jay. "Why'd you let 'em do that?" Jay was against the concept of pizza deliveries at his restaurant, but understood the circumstances.

"He used a cell phone. I didn't have anything to do with it. I was gonna call you over, but you were too busy romancing the stone." Hugh wiggled his ring finger.

"Now *that* is a girl I could marry."

Hugh shook his head. "Speaking of which, you want me to keep serving the groom when he comes up here?"

"Yeah, let him make a fool of himself. I'm going home. Make sure they clean up their shit before they leave."

"I'll do the best I can, Jaybo."

They exchanged half hugs and Jay exited through the door in his office.

§ § §

Early the next morning he returned to the restaurant and found a carnival of wreckage. Pizza boxes, mostly still full, were strewn across the floor. Beer bottles and champagne glasses were scattered throughout the room. Napkins were shredded and tossed as if someone had detonated a confetti grenade. Behind the bar, Hugh had swept and restocked, but it was barely noticeable. Jay lifted off his black cashmere sweater and untucked his T-shirt. He wheeled in an empty industrial trashcan from the kitchen, grabbed a broom and began the unenviable task of clean-up. While sweeping up a slice of once-bitten pepperoni, he felt something solid slide underneath the bristles of the broom. He lifted it up and found Maddy's jewel-encrusted wedding ring. He dusted it off gently with the corner of his shirt and brought it to his office, stowing it safely on a shelf. Then he returned to his drudgery for another ninety minutes. By noon, he was worn out and covered in a thin film of last night's party. His shirt and jeans were discolored by sweat, food and dirt. Fortunately, lunch was not served on Sunday and Maison did not open until five. Jay washed his hands thoroughly and sauntered to the kitchen to fix a sandwich. He then returned to the bar and filled a glass with ice, and root beer from the fountain.

"Hello? Is anybody in here?"

Jay had just taken an enormous bite of roast beef on a baguette and a smidge of horseradish mayo had dripped down the side of his chin. At that moment, Madison appeared in the doorway. She was wearing a velvety, baby blue Juicy Couture sweatsuit with a pair of Puma running sneakers to match. Jay realized that he had forgotten to relock the side door after throwing the garbage in the dumpster outside. Instinctually, he began chewing and swallowing with the voracity of a competitive eater midway through his challenge. It felt like five minutes had passed before he could respond coherently. He took a gulp of soda and wiped his mouth.

"Hey, I wasn't expecting anyone."

"Clearly," Maddy smiled, poking fun at Jay's haggard appearance. "Sorry about the mess last night. I hope you didn't have to clean it all up yourself."

Jay was beyond saving face. "Oh, yeah. No worries. The cleaners just left. Matter of fact, I was just coming back from church…"

This time, Maddy laughed uncontrollably. Jay was captivated by her smile but did not understand the broader contextual undertones that made his statement so amusing.

"Owww. Now I feel bad." Giggles erupted once again. "You just came from church? Oh, that's too funny."

"Would you like a sandwich or something? Glass of soda?" Jay didn't dare touch his own food.

"Actually, a diet Coke would be great."

He filled her glass and handed her a straw. "Excuse me for a second."

Jay returned with her ring in a small cloth.

"You must be looking for this?"

They exchanged mild pleasantries while Maddy finished her soda. Then, as she was walking away, Jay longingly and guiltily gazed at her curvaceous backside.

Later that evening, he began asking people who she was and where she came from. Community gossipers were eager to tell him her "story," but very few actually knew much about it. Maddy and Jay had both graduated high school in 1989. Since Jay had attended schools outside of Lenox from the time he was thirteen all the way through college, he had only heard rumors about this "hot chick" who had moved into town and was brainwashed by a religious cult. But Madison did not fit the description of a traditional hometown girl gone wayward, and for the next few months, the image of her stayed with him.

CHAPTER 14

For their honeymoon, Julian took Madison to Maui to learn how to windsurf. Growing up in a small beach town in Australia, he had started windsurfing shortly after he learned how to walk. Maddy picked up the sport so quickly it aggravated Julian, and throughout their ten-day trip he peppered her with hostile, condescending quips.

When they returned to California, Julian announced that they were moving to London. This was good news for Maddy, who had grown bored playing the roll of a San Francisco hausfrau. In preparation, she began reading *Tatler* magazine and watching *Absolutely Fabulous* reruns on Comedy Central. She joined the Pacific Heights health club and hired a personal trainer. Julian's intentions were to relocate to London temporarily while he worked on an acquisition of a microcap biotech company, so he arranged an extended stay at the Berkeley Hotel in Knightsbridge.

Maddy was particularly excited because Harrods was only a short walk away.

As soon as Julian revealed his intentions to work abroad, his docket of deals in the United States dried up. This translated into more face time with his wife, and fewer of his volatile mood swings. During the day, Maddy's sole responsibility was choosing a restaurant for dinner. She embraced this as a challenge, and using the ratings system in Zagats she selected a myriad of eateries all over the area. They ate at Aqua, Chez Panisse, The Slanted Door and Gary Danko. They ate Japanese in Union Square, seafood on the Wharf, Greek in the Mission, Cuban in the Castro, CaliMex in Lower Height, and Peruvian downtown. Julian would crack the occasional quip about "mingling with riff-raff" but he was generally amicable about trying new foods in different neighborhoods. This would be the high point of their marriage.

When they got to London, Julian began working virtually nonstop, and with his schedule, his venomous temper returned. Maddy quickly discovered it was best to stay out of his way until the weekend. To compensate, she pampered herself at the hotel spa until it grew dull. Twice a week she got a manicure, pedicure, massage and facial, and most mornings she swam in the pool and read magazines in the sauna before returning to the master suite for a specially prepared brunch. Living in a hotel did not give her opportunities to purchase furnishings or artwork, so she "redecorated" her wardrobe at least twice a month. Other than shopping and an occasional Saturday night out with Julian, Madison rarely left the hotel. After a few months of only minimal social interactions, a bitter, confining loneliness began to spin a cocoon around her psyche. With the passing of each day, the solitude and social anxieties intensified. With an idle mind, she began reliving unsettling memories of incremental brainwashing and a botched deprogramming. She lay in bed with the shades drawn, feeling hollow, numb and disconnected. Her sickness became psychosomatic. She gained weight, and became too self-conscious to leave the room. This cycle lasted for nearly two months.

One afternoon, Maddy was lying in bed with her head buried under a pillow. The phone next to the bed was ringing intrusively. A full sixty seconds passed before she finally lifted up the receiver and promptly hung up to silence the clamor. One minute later it began ringing again. Maddy was frustrated. She lifted up the receiver.

"What?" she shouted.

"Is that how they answer the phone in England?"

Maddy sprung up. The familiarity of Rachel's voice was instantly comforting.

"Rothstein!"

"How ARE you?"

A sterile pause gave Rachel a window to Maddy's mind state.

"Madison, pull up the shades and get out of bed! I'm coming to London!"

This was just the incentive she needed. The next morning she woke up at ten-thirty and ventured downstairs for a swim, a steam and a sauna. She got a manicure and pedicure, and later that afternoon she put on a new outfit and meandered into the Blue Bar for a drink.

A man dressed in a perfectly tailored, charcoal pinstriped suit was perched at the other end of the bar. He wore a pale pink dress shirt and a white necktie spotted with pale pink polkadots. A ruffled pocket square that matched the pattern on his tie was tucked into the front pocket of his suit coat. His hair was slicked back with styling mousse, completing the look of an over-the-hill Versace model. He stared unabashedly at Maddy, who noticed him without looking back. Although still self-conscious, Maddy enjoyed the attention, sipping her drink as if she were Lauren

Bacall in *To Have and Have Not*. Finally, as she was swirling the last remnants of her second martini, the man walked over. His voice was a smooth tenor, and his European accent was as thick as it was indistinct.

"American girls always drink their martinis with vodka, when a proper martini is made with gin."

Maddy was tongue-tied, as indeed her martini was mixed with Grey Goose vodka, extra dry vermouth and a drop of olive juice. Simultaneously, each acknowledged the other's matrimonial jewels. With a dash of arrogance, he lifted up her martini glass and signaled the bartender.

"She will have what I was having."

He retrieved his drink and sat down next to her, cupping a small handful of salted nuts and dropping them in his mouth one at a time. The bartender gingerly set her new drink on a glossy, marble coaster.

Slightly off balance, Maddy ad libbed. "And how would you know I was drinking a vodka martini?"

He stood up and placed his left arm around her opposite shoulder so that the corner of her ear was grazing the lapel of his blazer.

"Look at the color. Gin is a very translucent liquor, while vodka is quite cloudy."

They looked the same to her. Neverthe-less, Maddy enjoyed the subtle aroma of his Burberry cologne.

"Cigarette?" He pulled out two cigarettes from a gold case that was inside his coat pocket.

Maddy had resisted smoking her entire life until this moment, but reached for the cigarette daintily with her thumb and index finger. He ignited his smoke with a vintage Dupont lighter, using the burning ember to light Maddy's.

"Fritz Vandeveld," he said. A quick cloud of smoke escaped his mouth and he sucked it back fluidly. "Are you going to drink your drink or simply allow it to gather dust?"

Maddy shook his hand, trying to ignore the harshness of the tobacco as she inhaled.

"Nice to meet you." She did not offer her name but the bartender blew her cover.

"Mrs. Bixby, the kitchen would like to know if you will be having anything pre-pared for lunch before they switch to the din-ner menu?"

"That's OK, Thomas. Thank you. I'll be eating with my husband later this evening." Not true, but she wanted to project the illu-sion of being wealthy and unapproachable. Fritz took the bait.

"Mrs. Bixby? I suppose, then, that this is not your first night at the Berkeley."

Madison found her conversational rhythm. "Just as this is not my first gin martini."

The twinkle in Fritz's eyes revealed a mounting sense of intrigue.

"What's a ravishing American girl doing in this vapid chalet?"

Even after months of depression and reclusion, Maddy was too sharp, too charismatic to be submissively charmed.

"First, Fritz, only my Daddy has permission to refer to me as a girl. And second, I live at this vapid chalet, so you best watch your tongue next time you speak ill of my surroundings." Maddy smiled and looked away, exhaling a narrow stream of smoke.

Fritz paused to adjust his necktie as his expression sobered ever so slightly. "Methinks the lady doth protest too much."

Maddy sipped her drink unaffectedly and tapped her cigarette on the ashtray. Fritz wrote his room number on a cocktail napkin, folded it up and slid it down the bar.

"When I am in London, that is where I stay. So, you see, this is also *my* vapid chalet." Maddy found his accent both sexy and comforting. However, as she took the last sip of her drink, she dabbed her lips with the napkin, and without opening it, dropped it into the empty glass.

"If you will excuse me, my husband will be home shortly and I don't like to keep him waiting."

Again, far from the truth, but she was peddling the image of the devoted wife. Almost metaphorically, she left her cigarette smoking in the ashtray and leisurely glided out of the room, resisting the urge to gaze back.

Fritz was left standing with an idle grin. He understood this to mean he would need to make some adjustments in his approach next time he encountered Mrs. Bixby.

CHAPTER 15

Night has fallen on I-95. A torrential downpour earlier in the afternoon causes steam to rise from the highway. Smitty is behind the wheel and Jay reclines in the passenger seat. A one-hitter with a heavy coat of resin sits smoking in the cup holder, as both travelers are too stoned to take another hit. Axl has been lulled to sleep by Jay's hair-band ballads and a hot-boxed high.

They pass fireworks superstores, truck stop buffets and sprawling tobacco farms, all indications of reaching South Carolina. Jay's voice has gotten raspy from telling his story. Smitty had been driving for the past four hours. At the next rest area plaza, they pull over to walk around and refuel. Axl does not stir in their absence.

While Jay pumps gas, Smitty stocks up on fireworks at the MobileMart. Back at the Range Rover, Jay pulls out a regulation size football and when Smitty spots Jay clutching the pigskin, he instinctively "goes long." After a few minutes of parking lot heroics, an old Ford F-150 with a confederate flag plate decal comes careening around the bend. A gang of rowdy adolescents packed into the rear cab and seemingly under the influence shout obscenities at the plaza patrons.

"Hey! You bunch of fuckin' diddlers! Weer comin' fur you, fuckwads! Gamecocks rule the roost!"

As the truck passes, Smitty notices a faded bumper sticker that reads: *I'd Rather Be Shootin' Yankees.*

He is amused and mildly frightened. "Let's get the fuck out of here before we get hogtied and gang-raped."

"I'm right behind you, Smit," Jay concurs. "I'll drive."

On the road again, they break out into spontaneous impersonations.

"Git 'er dunn, fuckwads!"

"Pick up yur skirt Nancy-boy, this ain't no sqirr dance."

"Heeeehawww. Gamecocks, fucker!"

"What the hell is a gamecock anyway?"

"A fighting hen, I suppose. Team mascot, state bird... I don't fuckin' know. How long until we get to my folks' crib?"

Jay rolls his eyes. "My guess is four hours."

"We're fucked. Might as well roll another dube." Smitty reaches for the sack. "Go on, Jay, keep spinnin' yur yarn."

CHAPTER 16

The truth about Maddy is that she really did *seem* wealthy and unapproachable. She'd studied the culture and learned the mannerisms of the elite; she knew all of the dos and don'ts in shopping and socializing; had the conversational banter down to the pronunciation and intonations of particular words. But deep down, Maddy was a fragile, self-conscious girl who barely knew herself. Consequently, she could never really synthesize the aspects of her life that brought her happiness, nor could she analyze the elements that contributed to her depression. To a great extent, she ignored the complexities of her own character, acknowledging only the most primitive symptoms of loneliness and despondency. Having unlearned her mother's reclusive tendencies as a child, she had inadvertently rediscovered them as an adult. Her experiences with Faith First forever tainted her perception of people, and throughout her life she remained especially wary of benevolent intentions.

Rachel was an ideal friend for Madison. She was comforting without being overbearing, and genuinely kind without being unrealistic. The week she came for a vacation was the happiest Maddy had known since moving to London. Together they visited the Tate; caught a play on the West End; toured Buckingham Palace, and took a boat trip on the Thames. On Rachel's last night, they were sitting in the Blue Bar having a drink when Maddy heard the voice of an indistinct tenor.

"Shame, shame. You're having a pillow fight party and did not invite me."

As he approached, Rachel was getting ready to extend the man some New York-flavored epithets, but Maddy interjected.

"That's OK, Rach, Fritz is a friend of mine. He just has trouble remembering his manners when he's around women."

"How delightful," he continued. "You've persuaded a little American friend for a pond hop, have you?"

Rachel was heating up. "Who the hell is this guy, Madison?"

Although she hadn't mentioned him to Rachel, she had been thinking about him ever since the night they met. She even tore off a Burberry cologne ad from *Tatler* magazine and rubbed it on her wrist.

"Fritz Vandeveld." He put out his hand graciously. Rachel extended her pinky and Fritz lifted it up and kissed it.

"Are you fucking serious?" Rachel was far more appalled than charmed, but Maddy found his glib mannerisms oddly appealing.

Fritz picked up their bar tab before adjourning to his room and Rachel gave Maddy her frank opinion.

"He's a cheesy narcissist. I'm sorry, but he is. I don't care how much money he has, he's creepy and *you're* married!"

Madison respected Rachel's opinion, more so than anyone, but Rachel was leaving the next day and her sway over Maddy's childlike impulses was null and void. Although Maddy knew very little about her own proclivities toward men, she had a keen sense of what she desired; and to her, Fritz was the antithesis of Julian. He was dignified and gracious, handsome and erudite and albeit refined, personable and even somewhat goofy. He exuded a harmlessly pompous charm that Maddy found particularly endearing. She was most attracted to the simplest attributes like the touch of his butter-soft hands, and of course, the subtle scent of his distinctly masculine fragrance.

Maddy began lingering in the Blue Bar at odd hours. This gave her a new opportunity to socialize and polish her appearance. Since Fritz was also married, Maddy was relieved to shed all pretensions about the nature of the attraction. To Madison, "having an affair" was a glamorously illicit celebrity trend, which was as thrilling as it was morally compromising. Julian's work schedule was generous in this respect.

At first, their barstool dialogue remained quid pro quo. With sex as her bargaining tool, Maddy wanted to have some fun with Fritz before she actually severed her marital vows.

On Thanksgiving Day, Julian left for a two-week business excursion in Switzerland and Maddy met Fritz at the Blue Bar midafternoon. As he approached, he smiled suggestively, displaying his chalky white teeth.

"What's with the harlequin grin?" Maddy asked.

He kissed her on both cheeks. "How would you like to have dinner with me in Istanbul, Persia?"

"You mean Turkey?"

"Yes, of course. It is Thanksgiving, is it not?" He put his hand on her shoulder.

"Very cute." Maddy removed his hand from her shoulder.

"I'm serious, my dear. I have a cozy bungalow just off the Byzantine Harbor. There is a plane waiting for us. We can be there in a few hours and you'll be back in your little bedroom upstairs in time for breakfast—if you wish." He slid his hand down her arm and then gripped her waist.

"You're really serious, aren't you?"

With his other hand, he tilted her head so she could see the sincerity in his eyes. "Quite so."

Maddy politely declined the invitation, claiming she wanted to spend the day basking in American nostalgia, which, in a hotel room in England, consisted of eating turkey and cranberry sauce, watching *Home Alone* on the movie channel and drifting off into a "tryptophan coma." The actual reason Maddy did not go to Istanbul was that she was not cosmetically prepared. Fritz extended the same invitation for the following day and Maddy promised to "sleep on it."

Early the next morning she got a bikini wax, a French massage and a mani/pedi. She ate brunch in the dining area instead of her room. Fritz eventually joined her at the table. He ordered two mimosas and posed the question again.

"So, I trust you are completely satiated by your philistine fodder."

"Philistine fodder? I hope you are not referring to Macaulay Culkin."

"I do not know who this is. But you are rested?"

"I am."

"Good. So you will accompany me this afternoon?"

"I would love to," Maddy replied with a twinkle.

"Perfect. I will have the plane ready by noon."

"I will just need to pack a bag." Maddy chewed on the stem of a maraschino cherry.

"Nonsense, we will get you everything you need when we land."

She liked the sound of that.

§   §   §

The Vandevelds were one of the wealthiest and most influential families in Belgium. For nearly two centuries they had owned and operated shipping ports throughout the Netherlands. Fritz's two eldest brothers jointly managed the business, and while Fritz was also a rightful heir to the fortune he was never allowed to become an equal partner. Given his aristocratic background, Fritz was polished and well educated, but for all intents and purposes was considered the family jester. After an unsuccessful bid as a politician, his mother found him a job as Belgium's commerce ambassador to Great Britain. It was an innocuous position, demanding little more than the stamping of his surname on global export transactions. Fritz, however, found other business opportunities using his status as a diplomat.

With a generational knowledge of international shipping, he also became England's largest supplier of hashish and raw MDMA, the chemical used to make Ecstasy. He was the "unaffiliated" point man in a massive drug-trafficking operation that netted him over seven million tax-free Euros annually. He remained both nameless and faceless, merely connecting the right people and accepting incremental payouts with no paper trail. Although he enjoyed the risk and intrigue of overseeing a drug cartel, his involvement was not for the money. As the youngest of three boys, this was his way of thumbing his nose at familial neglect.

His wife, Christiana, was the granddaughter of a former Belgian prime minister and their marriage had been "arranged" when she was twenty-two years old. His two children, Lamar and Anna, thirteen and sixteen respectively, were being groomed for political careers of their own and Christiana constantly warned Fritz that although the children bore his family's name, they carried the reputation of their father. This was her way of reminding him that she was not naïve about his lengthy pedigree of affairs and liaisons, but, for the sake of their children, she demanded his discretion.

§   §   §

Istanbul marked a turning point for Madison Bixby. The trip itself lasted five days and four nights. Once they had slept together Maddy relinquished both her coyness and her bargaining chips. Fritz, who turned fifty the day they flew back to London, embraced her with a gentle fondness she grew to covet. Over the next month, they spent virtually every night together, and when they were apart Maddy longed for his presence. Yet the more she opened to the prospect of real romance, the more Fritz pulled back. Their relationship was as covert as his narcotics dealings. While he would court women openly, as he did with Madison, he was adept at limiting the evidence for speculation. Occasionally, Dutch paparazzi would follow him around and Maddy would have to hide in the car or the hotel room until the cameras were gone.

At first, Maddy and Fritz bonded intrinsically, as they were both the youngest children of neglectful families. He had a playful nature about him and behind closed doors they shared a special goofiness that was genuinely reassuring and helped her alleviate the moral conundrum of cheating on her husband. But as time passed, the context of their relationship shifted. As a man twenty years her senior, Maddy found herself more attracted to his elderly influence than his fading, debonair charm. Since her own father never nurtured her as a young girl, Fritz became as much of a paternal figure as he was a lover. Gradually, the intangible grip of dependency grabbed Maddy and she began making idle innuendos about how their lives would be so much easier if neither were married.

§   §   §

Julian decided that once the biotech deal was complete, the Bixbys would be moving back to San Francisco. This was a devastating revelation. Maddy had just returned from a week in Fiji with Fritz and Julian's announcement blindsided her, so much so she could not temper her reaction. It was a bustling Friday night at Criterion, a French brasserie in the Piccadilly section of London, and Maddy burst into tears mid-course. Unable to contain her weeping, she excused herself from the table and scurried toward the loo. Julian unaffectedly cut his steak without so much as glance in her direction.

Maddy broke the news to Fritz at the Bilderberg Garden Hotel in Amsterdam a week later. Fritz had been married for thirty-two years, only two of which were monogamous, and he knew inner workings of an affair the way a jewel thief knows the blueprint of his next heist. He sensed her vulnerability from the moment they met at the airport. Inside the hotel room, Maddy could barely force the words from her mouth. Fritz stroked her hair gently, but as the momentum of sadness grew in her voice, she began stuttering and sobbing and Fritz bumped up the volume of the television set to mask the sound.

She launched into a hysterical lament, pleading for him to leave his wife and threatening consequences if he did not.

"I won't be able to do this anymore," she kept repeating as she gasped for air. Double speak was a habit she had artfully cultivated over the last six months while deceiving her husband, and Fritz understood "this" implied her own life and not merely the existence of their relationship. Albeit sympathetic, he was unwaveringly steadfast. He attempted to comfort her for nearly two hours, but she was inconsolable. Although the room was registered under a faux surname, he feared paparazzi would flock like hungry pigeons to the sound of a woman's wailing.

While Maddy was in the bathroom wrapping ice cubes into washcloths and dabbing her eyes to reduce the swelling, Fritz made a discreet exit. He left twelve hundred Euros on the bureau, quietly phoned his driver and slipped out of the hotel unnoticed. When Maddy came out and realized that he was gone, her legs buckled and her body cascaded into a pile on the red plush carpet. She was too tired to cry and too sad to feel sorry. She lay slumped sideways in a white sequin robe, with her cheek pressed firmly against the floor, shamefully staring at her reflection in the mirror on the back of the bathroom door.

CHAPTER 17

Smitty has been scrolling through Jay's music library. Finally, click, click goes the iPod and Smitty looks up at Jay. Clenching his fist as if he were gripping a microphone, he begins singing along.

"I was a highwayman. Along the coach roads I did ride. With sword and pistol by my side. Many a young maid lost her baubles to my trade... Many a soldier shed his life blood on my blade... The bastards hung me in the spring of twenty-five... But I am still alive..."

It's late and Jay is rubbing his eyes while steering with his knees. He shakes his head disapprovingly.

"You're so fucked, it's beyond belief."

"...I was a dam builder. Across the river deep and wide... I'm a little disappointed you are not appreciating the significance of this tune."

"Oh, I get it, douchebag, we're the fucking highwaymen. But it's three-fifteen in the morning and I'm tired as shit."

"Do you want me to drive?"

"No. But do you recognize any of this?

Are we getting close to your folks' place? Because if not, that Comfort Inn up ahead looks pretty fucking sweet."

Smitty glares back. "Good one. You almost had me."

A steamy night fog has blanketed the roads, making it difficult to see beyond the narrow beam of the headlights. Smitty lowers the volume of the iPod with a counter-clockwise twist of his index finger. He senses Jay's frustration.

"Look buddy, all I know is that from I-95, you take the exit heading toward Bluffton/Hilton Head. What's wrong with your GPS?"

Jay sighs with heightened exasperation. "Do you recall that you couldn't remember your parents' address? Do you remember not wanting to call your wife to look it up because you didn't want to 'deal' with her when you were high?"

Smitty reaches into the glove compartment and pulls out a small bag of Smartfood popcorn. Axl rattles his collar and barks a few times, signaling that he needs a bathroom stop. Jay is teetering on the brink of detonation. He flicks on the right turning signal and slows the car toward the side of the road. Smitty tears open the bag and dumps a handful of kernels in his mouth.

"Have you lost your mind? It's the middle of the night and we're lost in the deep South driving a Range Rover with Mass plates. Haven't you seen *Deliverance*?"

"Well, what the fuck do you want me to do? My dog needs to drop a deuce. Who knows how far we still have to go, and I could use a piss."

"You could use a piss," Smitty chides. "Here," extending his snack bag, "eat some *Smart*food, dumbass."

The car has come to a stop but the blinker is still flickering. Jay stares out at the road. "Do you think it's better to leave the lights on or off?"

"On dude. Leave 'em on. And hurry the fuck up."

"Do you think maybe I should put on the hazards?"

"Just go!"

In a delayed reaction, Jay hops out and walks around the vehicle to open the back door for the dog. Once freed, Axl leaps onto dirt and sprints into the woods. Smitty reclines in the passenger seat, anxiously nibbling on his popcorn.

Jay is watering a nearby tree trunk and Axl is rummaging in the brush. A sharp beam of light slices its way into the hazy hindsight. Both Jay and Smitty turn at the same time.

Smitty powers down his window and calls out into the night: "Yo, Gordon. Whaddya say we get the fuck out of here?"

"Axl!" Jay yells, but his dog is busy pawing and sniffing the brush. The orbs of light are expanding as they draw closer.

"Axl! C'mon boy!" Jay hears Axl digging. "This fucking dog!"

Smitty is fixated on the sideview mirror. "Holy fuck! It's a Mack truck!" Jay heads into the woods. The truck slows, only a few hundred yards away.

"Oh, Christ. It's ass-raping time." Smitty powers up his window and slithers down in his seat as the twelve-wheeler approaches. Jay lets out a deep-throated groan.

"Ouch!!! Goddammit!!!" Wearing flip-flops and shorts, he runs directly through a bramble patch.

"Axl! Get over here!"

Axl comes galloping through the trees. The truck has put on its right turning signal. As it inches past the Range Rover, the driver blows the horn and the sound bellows in the fog like a steam engine at sea. Smitty tilts his head up. The truck stops on the side of the road and Jay is limping back to the car with Axl panting at his heels. As he reaches the pavement, the headlights of the Range Rover reveal scrapes and blood on his lower leg. Limping to the back, he opens the door and Axl leaps into the car. Smitty taps on the window, motioning for Jay to pick up his pace. The driver has stepped down from the truck and is walking toward them. Jay gets as far as the driver's side door but stops short.

A slender silhouette steps into view wearing a light denim vest and a mesh baseball hat with a long bill.

"Do y'all need any help?" It is the voice of middle-aged woman. She pauses by the hood of the car and they notice the long blond ponytail tucked behind her hat.

Jay speaks loudly, over the sound of the truck engine. "No thanks, my dog just had to go number two."

"That's more information than I was looking for. I just noticed your car there and thought you might be in some sort of trouble, it being so late and all."

"No, we're OK."

Smitty powers down the window. "How you doing, ma'am?"

"Just fine," the woman replies.

Jay looks at him in bewilderment.

"You mind if I ask you how far till we reach Hilton Head?"

"Hilton Head? Y'all passed that, I'd say, a hundred miles ago."

She notices Jay's leg. "Good lord. That's

quite a scratch, son. There's a First Aid kit in the truck. You're welcome to it."

"Oh, that's OK. I'll be fine." Jay gets into the car, which is still blinking.

"You boys have a good night then."

"Thank you."

"Thanks a lot."

Jay slams the door and straps on his seat belt.

"You got any more of that Smartfood?"

"Christ, Jay."

"Don't even fucking start. Everything is fine."

"Fine? Under your leadership we missed the exit a hundred miles ago!"

Jay pulls out on to the road, and as he is passing the truck the woman holds up a finger. He taps the breaks.

Under his breath, Smitty protests. "Now what?"

Jay powers down his window.

She raises her voice but it is muffled by her engine.

"Hold on a minute." She hops up into the truck and reaches for something on the seat.

"Floor it, Gordy. This could be that chick from *Monster*."

She motions for Smitty to roll down his window. He hesitatingly obliges.

"You boys look like you might be able to

get some use out of these." From her window, she dangles a five-pack of Budweiser cans strung together by a plastic holder.

They both look at each other and shrug. As Smitty stretches his arms out she drops the cans down into his hands.

He puts up his thumb signaling their appreciation. The woman raises a can of Bud as if to toast "the highwaymen" on their trip.

"Careful not to spill," she yells out with a smile as she takes a sip.

Jay waves politely as they drive away, and Smitty pops open a beer.

"Huh. That was... odd. And slightly troubling."

"Gimme one of those." Jay glances into the rear view and notices the truck pulling back onto road. "She was sort of attractive, too."

Smitty pops open a second can and hands it to Jay. "I'd bang her."

"I'd definitely bang her."

Jay turns up the volume and replays the song on the iPod.

Smitty interjects. "Uh, I hate to ruin the moment, but we're going the wrong way."

Jay shakes his head. "Oh no. The Comfort Inn is just up the road."

Smitty is unmotivated to argue.

"I was a sailor. I was born amongst the tide..." They both know the words to Johnny Cash's "Highwayman," and they sing along with uninspired gusto, periodically sipping their beers.

"...By the sea I did abide... I sailed a schooner 'round the horn to Mexico..."

A smile creeps onto Jay's brow.

Smitty stops singing. "What?"

"Nothing."

"No, what is it?"

"That was her maiden name."

"Who? Femme fatale?"

Jay nods. "Madison Horn."

"No offense, Jay, but this chick sounds completely nuts. But you always go for that *Girl Interrupted* type, don't you?"

"Yeah, but this one was a few strokes over par, even for me."

"I'm not sure what that means, but cheers." They clink their cans and chug, as Johnny Cash's verse drones on with baritone bravado:

"I'll fly a starship... across the universe divide. And when reach the other side... I'll find a place to rest my spirit if I can... Perhaps I'll become a highwayman again..."

CHAPTER 18

Maddy woke up on the floor in her room at the Bilderberg. From the shadows on the carpet, she could tell that morning had forced its way through the drapes. She was shivering. Her head was pounding. Her eyes were swollen, her hair was straggly and her body ached. She had only a blurry recollection of last night and could not at all remember what triggered the heartrending hysteria.

She rolled onto her stomach and lay there for a few seconds, gathering her breath. Then, gradually bending her torso, she lifted to her knees, pushing her bunched robe to the back. Finally, as if the referee was on his nine-count, Madison, whose first breath of life occurred during the most celebrated moments of boxing history, sprung to her feet.

As a Pisces, her conflicted pride and stubborn complacency sometimes outweighed her compassion and ambition. Yet, whenever her toughness was truly tested she always found the inner resolve of Ali/ Frazier. She stumbled toward the bathroom and literally gasped when she saw her reflection in the mirror on the door. Standing at the sink, she flipped down the glossy brass knob on the right and a stream of cold water gushed from the gasket. Fumbling through her travel bag, she pulled out an electric toothbrush and a small tube of Simply White Aquafresh toothpaste. The shrill hum of spinning bristles was oddly comforting and the icy mint shattered the stagnant dryness of her mouth. When she was finished, she cupped two handfuls of water and splashed them on her face with pitiless vigor. Then she let her robe slither to the limestone floor and reached inside the shower, adjusting the lever until the temperature was perfectly steamy.

She stood under the sprinkler jets for several minutes without moving. Eventually she lathered a loofah sponge with lavender soap and exfoliated her entire body. After showering, it took her a full hour to primp herself until she was publicly presentable. Like a Roman soldier gearing for battle, her outfit was body armor, protecting her from the piercing gaze of perception. She wore an extra layer of makeup, a pink tweed Chanel suit and her usual oversized designer sunglasses. She exited the hotel wheeling her suitcase and was particularly careful not to tilt her head in either direction, as any subtle movement would reveal her puffy eyelids behind the large, dark lenses.

The hotel provided a car service to Schiphol Airport, on the outskirts of Amsterdam, and Maddy used the currency Fritz had left to cover her expenses.

From her window seat on a business class flight to Heathrow, she stared through her shades into an empty gray horizon. This harkened a memory of lying with Jed on lawn chairs, gazing at a hazy summer sky from their black-tar rooftop in Manhattan. She smiled, recalling the simplicity of her life at that time. In this moment, Maddy came to the realization that the thrill of affluence and the projection of status had fueled her lifeblood for so long it had eclipsed the individualism she once prided herself on when she was young. The actual proposition of leaving Julian did not enter her conscious mind on the flight to London, but a subconscious seed was planted.

When she returned to the Berkeley, the familiar scent and claustrophobic layout of the hotel room was, for the first time, suffocating. Somehow, Maddy longed for her old bike, the feeling of soft wind in her hair and a tangy apple Blow Pop on her tongue. She began taking walks around the city and soon the walks became all-day excursions. She discovered the vast serenity of Covent Gardens and the many artisan markets at Piccadilly Circus. She studied a few Underground Tube maps and occasionally rode the Piccadilly Line from Knightsbridge to Paddington. She bought a digital camera at Harrods and began snapping frivolous pictures of Tower Bridge, Big Ben and the River Thames. One afternoon she strolled to the city and laughed aloud when she came upon the oddly shaped "Gherkin" building, named for its pickle likeness. Instinctively she dug out her cell phone and called Rachel.

"My God. This stubby, unsightly tower looks just like my husband's penis!"

Rachel was relieved to hear Maddy in good spirits.

"Gross," she chuckled. "I'm sure you're not the first person to make that observation."

"Well, excuse me. Brits are perverts! I mean, who *erects* a building that looks like this?"

"Did you just make a pun?"

Maddy looked up and felt a pellet of rain plummet from the heavens.

"Shit, Rach! It's about to pour on me. I'll call you later."

§   §   §

Before leaving London, Fritz rang the hotel a few times and she spoke to him over the phone, exchanging charming pleasantries, but neither acknowledged the circumstances of their last encounter. As a result, Fritz did not return to England until Maddy had moved back to San Francisco.

CHAPTER 19

To inaugurate the Bixby's California homecoming, Julian bought a low-rise building in Pacific Heights. He began renovations immediately, converting the entire structure into a three-floor townhouse with a rooftop garden and a glass ceiling solarium. He ordered a bevy of new furniture: dressers, cabinets, bookshelves and tables made from exotic, endangered wood from India, Australia and New Zealand. Maddy, who had previously taken on the interior decorating responsibilities, was not even consulted about the layout of their new home. Similarly, Julian sold the Land Rover Defender to his personal assistant, Shelby. Maddy found this out when she went to pick up Julian's dry cleaning and the car was not in the garage.

"How am I supposed to get your clothes,

honey?" she later asked in a calm but condescending voice.

"Take the fucking Baht!" was his goaded
response.

"Why don't you have your assistant pick
up your dry cleaning, now that she has
my car? Or just make *her* take the fucking
BART!"

As Julian stormed out of the room, Maddy's eyes welled. "I'm your fucking wife!"

Then, randomly on a Wednesday night,
Julian did not return from work. At around
8:00 PM he instructed Shelby to call Maddy
at home and tell her that he had left for a golf
outing in Scotland and could not be reached
until Sunday night.

Maddy was more relieved than upset.

At one time, Maddy would have coveted
even the idea of living in an entire townhouse
in one of San Francisco's most affluent neighborhoods. But upward mobility at this stage
of her marriage was barely an afterthought.

While Julian was in Scotland, Maddy
bought herself a brand new burgundy Mercedes SLK350 Roadster using the cash balance in a joint brokerage account. She also
joined the 24-hour Fitness on Bryant Street,
which was a younger, more social gym than
the exclusive Health Club in Pacific Heights.
Although she was not outwardly seeking the

attention of another man, ulterior motives pointed her toward such possibilities.

When Julian learned that Maddy had used their money at Merrill Lynch to purchase her car, he promptly closed the account and fired his asset manager. In turn, Maddy stopped having sex with her husband.

While the new building was being converted, their old apartment became a pressure cooker. Movers were periodically packing and carting things to storage units. Real estate agents and property appraisers were constantly surveying the building and Maddy was often the unintentional intermediary between the broker and prospective buyer. The frenzy created additional strain on their already noxious interactions, adding an extra dose of circumstantial stress for Julian.

One afternoon, Julian stopped home from work to ensure the movers did not mishandle his precious West Australian jarrah timber dining room set. Maddy was supposed to be supervising but instead she sat on the floor of the bathroom fondly gazing at old photos of Fritz, which were strewn across the marble tiles. When Maddy heard the front door slam, she knew by the hollow thud of footsteps that it was her husband. With her forearm, she swept together the pictures and stuffed them into the shoebox, covertly placing a pair of unworn Jimmy Choo stilettos and tissue paper on top.

"Madison! Git the fuck down heah! You'ah supposed to be wotching these termyites."

He was referring to the movers. Maddy stuffed the shoebox into a suitcase and shut the hall closet gently. Then she tiptoed to the top of the stairs. Julian was hollering at one of the workers but when he saw Maddy he redirected his tirade. Normally, Maddy weathered his oral assaults until he cooled off or left, but on this afternoon he finally tested her inner resolve.

"You don't fucking werk…"

She put the ball of her foot on the first stair.

"You won't fuck me… "

His jowls turned crimson and his upper body gesticulated with fury.

"What the fuck are you good foah?"

Once again, as if it were a birthright, Maddy exhibited some of that heavyweight tenacity.

"Shut!!! The fuck!!! Up!!!" she screamed, and the shrill echo reverberated throughout the half-vacant apartment.

"You shut up, you fucking orphan!"

This struck a nerve. She took one step forward and then another, and another. The staircase creaked below her feet and she could feel the inevitability of each footstep. She approached her husband with maddening slowness.

"Listen to you." She spoke in a calm, patronizing tone, but her eyes were inflamed. "You think you're such a big swinging dick? What? Because you take little public companies private?"

She stood right under his neck and looked straight up at him so their eyes linked. She enunciated every syllable. "You're just a limp prick and a lousy fuck."

With the movers looking on in awkward disbelief, Julian spun to his left and grabbed the first thing he saw—an original Picasso drawing he had recently purchased at a Sotheby's auction. He heaved it violently at Maddy's feet. She hopped as the frame split and skidded across the hardwood. Then he went around the room, ripping her collection of artwork and fixtures from the walls and hurling them into a pile in the corner. Expensive sculptures and glass ornaments shattered as they bounced. Madison shrieked and rushed over to stop him but the former rugby player was blinded by his temper. As she grabbed him by his arms, he took her wrists and flung her to the floor. She landed with a loud thud and the back of her neck caught the stout table leg. Julian stormed out

of the room barking indecipherable obscenities. Maddy lay on the hardwood shaken up
but still entirely composed. One of the movers,
a long-haired Mexican who spoke no English,
hovered over her with his hand extended.

"I'm fine," she said with embarrassed
poise, and waved him off. The mover backed
off timidly as Maddy got up, still short of
breath. She slipped into the half bathroom by
the front entrance and shut the door behind
her. Moments later she emerged with her hair
tied in a makeshift knot. She plucked a hat
off the coatrack and put on her sunglasses,
exiting the apartment with an abrupt slam.

On the street, her eyes grew teary and she
blinked several times, fighting the feeling of
self-pity. The rich, northern Cali sun seared
the sidewalk as she strolled aimlessly toward
the Marina. Although she had always known
this would be the inevitable denouement, it
was hard for her to swallow the notion that
her second marriage was over.

CHAPTER 20

Axl furiously sniffs the well-trod carpeting of the Comfort Inn. Smitty drops his bag by the foot of the bed and rips off the flowery bedspread, which is the same pattern as the carpet and drapes. Jay is in the bathroom with the door closed and the fan on.

Smitty calls out to him. "How's it going in there?"

"Slowly but surely," he hollers back, slurping the last of his beer.

Smitty shakes his head.

"Jay, this is fucking rough, dude. This room smells like a combination of condoms and carpet cleaner."

Jay doesn't respond. A few minutes later he emerges from the bathroom with a towel wrapped around his wounded leg. He cracks another can, and with a timbering tumble, he plummets onto the bed.

"What are you doing, jackass?"

"What?"

"You're lying on the bedspread!"

"So?"

"Are you nuts? It's common knowledge these things never get washed at chain motels."

"Smitty, relax. I'll shower in the morning."

"C'mon. Please. Just take it off."

Jay reluctantly bounces up and swipes off the bedspread. "I didn't know you were so OCD."

Smitty seems relieved. "Those things are breeding grounds for germs and STDs. And this place must be the Kwik-E-Mart for local whores."

"Now how the fuck do you know that?"

"Jay. Seriously, look at where we are. If you're not a whore or a trucker, or two assholes who can't read a map, there is absolutely no reason to be here."

Both turn off their bedside lamps and crawl under the top covers, still wearing their clothes. Smitty dons a protective winter hat to shield his hair from the pillows.

"Well, goodnight Stanley."

"Goodnight Ollie. Looks like another fine mess you've gotten us into."

Four hours later, Smitty shakes Jay.

"Jay baby. Yo, Jaybo!"

Jay rolls over, groggy.

"Let's get the fuck outta here. I can't sleep. I keep thinking shit is crawling on me."

Jay sits up in bed and yawns. The morning sun is fighting its way into the room.

Jay is delirious. "You drive."

Axl has found his way onto the bed. He wakes up from the commotion, stretches to a sitting position and settles into a gratifying ear scratch.

While Smitty is checking out, Jay sits in the car preparing the one-hitter.

Smitty slips into the driver's seat.

In his Spicoli voice Jay extends the pipe. "Wake and bake, bro."

"Can I look at a map before we get high?"

"Yeah, it's right back—" Jay curls his arm behind the seat and pulls out an atlas.

"Where are we, again?"

"We're south." Jay closes his eyes and leans back.

"We need to start heading west."

"You wanna skip Hilton Head?" Jay is dismayed.

"We'll lose a full day if we go back."

"Right now, dude, I really don't care if it takes an extra week. Let's just drive somewhere, get breakfast, and figure out how we can knock around some golf balls."

Smitty is scrutinizing the map.

"If we take I-95 to—"

"Dude, you're killin' me. Just hit this."

Smitty grabs the pipe and lighter, takes a quick pull, exhales and hands it back to Jay without taking his eyes off the map.

In defiance, Jay powers his seat back and clasps his hands behind his head, squinting from the early sunrays.

Fatigue sets in. Lacking immediate direction, the travelers are sleep-deficient and incoherent. The road trip is now three days old, and despite the fact that nearly a quarter ounce of marijuana and a half bottle of Demerol are gone, they have yet to reach their first destination. Equally inarticulate, neither can decide on the right move. Ego saturates the atmosphere inside the Range Rover, mingling with the skunky funk of Canadian hydroponics. By default, Smitty begins driving due south and a stubborn quietness ensues.

CHAPTER 21

Julian put up little objection to Maddy's request for a legal separation. While the divorce was pending, Maddy asked for eight thousand dollars a month as financial restitution, as well as her Mercedes SLK350, which she had shipped to Lenox in her name. Julian agreed. She packed four large suitcases of mostly clothes, shoes, jewelry and makeup, and boarded a flight from San Francisco to Hartford.

Maddy arrived at her parent's house on a frigid Thursday evening in February. She had not talked to her family since the wedding eight months earlier. She pulled up in front of the house in a shiny, black Lincoln and the reflection of the car gleamed in the frozen snow. Jane was home alone, sitting at the bridge table in the dining room staring out the window at the icicle formations hanging from the gutter. When she saw her daughter emerge from the Town Car, she did not budge. Trailed by a small procession of luggage, Maddy hauled her bags to the front door with help from her driver, a Russian immigrant dressed in a black polyester suit. She rang the front doorbell a few times because she did not have a key, and finally her mother appeared in the front hall.

The lifeless expression on her mother's face unearthed a myriad of old emotions. Maddy took a deep breath as Jane unlatched the deadbolt and they embraced without speaking.

CHAPTER 22

On the strength of Maison's success, Jay Gordon, along with two partners, was opening Porter's, a 150-seat steakhouse at the top of Railroad Street in Great Barrington. Although he managed to avoid much of the monotonous grunt work associated with launching a restaurant, working hours were more strenuous than ever. In addition to running Maison, which was a twenty-minute drive from Porter's, he was immersed in an endless brigade of meetings and decisions regarding everything from the patterns on the barstools to the side dishes on the prix fixe menu. Jay divided fourteen hours a day between the two restaurants.

It was midmorning in late May and the gentle guitar plucking of the Scorpions' seminal ballad "Winds of Change" tingled in Jay's headphones as he jogged lethargically on the treadmill at Lenox Fitness. Exhausted from a late night at Porter's, he zoned out to the rhythm of his rapid footsteps. On the second level, all the cardio machines faced a panoramic window that overlooked Route 7, and from the west side of the road he noticed a topless burgundy Mercedes, paused at a traffic light, signaling left toward the club entrance. As the car got closer, he could see the silhouette of a woman dressed in a matching sweatsuit and lightly tinted driving shades. Her hair was pulled back behind her neck and she rested her elbow on the vacant window space of the SLK. Jay slowed the pace of the treadmill so his vision was not jarred.

In Berkshire County, the sight of a young, sophisticated female driving alone in an expensive car in the middle of the week was certainly atypical. Jay squinted, focusing his eyes on the Mercedes as it came to a stop in the parking lot. The woman got out and strutted carefully toward the gym, almost as if she suspected she was being watched. Then, abruptly, she spun 180 degrees and walked back to the car to grab her bag. As she turned, Jay recognized the face. His throat felt heavy and his heart rate increased. Full of nervous adrenaline, he bumped up the pace of his jog.

Madison Bixby emerged from the women's locker room twenty minutes later. Jay saw her through the mirror by the free weights but was too intimidated to approach her. By her expression, he sensed that she had a busy mind and a heavy heart. His first thought was that her marriage had failed, but she was still wearing that same Harry Winston on her ring finger.

Jay spent an extra hour at the gym that day. He kept trying to find the right moment to reintroduce himself, but the opportunity never presented itself. Later that night at Maison, Jay sat in his usual spot at the bar, prodding Hugh with questions about the Horn family. Hugh, who was a veritable "page six" of Berkshire gossip, had not heard about Madison or any potential divorce. Jay asked him to tap his sources for information. Over the next week, Jay went to the gym each day. He kept his sport bag in the backseat of his silver Audi S4 sedan, and on a few occasions, he circled the parking lot looking for Maddy's Mercedes. If he saw her car, he would go exercise, but if not, he would come back later. This went on for several days, until he learned her routine well enough to coincide each visit. Yet he still had not found the chutzpah to talk to her. Slowly he grew aggravated with himself, and finally he decided to just ask her out. The night before the big day, he sat at the bar drinking Rudd Estate Cabernet and chatting with Hugh.

"So, what's the word on what we talked about?"

Hugh leaned in. "All I know is that she came to town in a car service with a whole bunch of luggage."

Jay scratched his chin. "Hmm. Not a typical move for a happy housewife."

Hugh shrugged.

"But that fucking ring. Why is she still wearing that ring?"

"I think it's a sentimental decoy, Jay. Think about it. She was married less than a year ago. Girls don't like to admit defeat so quickly, especially when it involves taking off a big fat rock. It's just her safety net, dude."

Jay nodded at Hugh's reasoning. "Here's the deal. I'll feel her out tomorrow when I reintroduce myself. If it goes well, I'll ask her to dinner. And if she says yes, I'll know the marriage is basically over."

Hugh put out his fist and Jay touched it. "But if she says no and uses her marriage as an excuse, I'll sell my restaurants and move to Mexico."

"Sounds like a solid plan."

"You gotta admit, it's pretty shady to ask a woman to join you for dinner when she's still wearing a giant diamond."

Hugh smiled broadly. "What did we used to say in high school? If she's worth having, she's worth taking?"

"Yeah, whatever. I'm not into taking other

peoples wives. The only reason I'm gonna to do this is because I *know* she is either separated or divorced. I mean, you remember her wedding night."

Hugh acknowledged Jay's reasoning with a reassuring wink. "Make it happen, Jay-baby."

Jay sighed. "She just looks so sad every time I see her. So I bring her flowers and buy her dinner, make her feel better. That's not a big deal, right?"

"I don't see the harm in it. Matter of fact, I think it would be wrong not to do it."

The next day he timed his workout perfectly. When he got to the club, Maddy was already there. He changed quickly and scampered upstairs to the second floor and took a few breaths before casually walking through the double doors. He spotted Maddy immediately in the corner of the room, stretching on the yoga mats. He waited until she stood up, and without hesitating he began walking toward her as if he was headed to the Smith machines. Their eyes met and Jay stopped short.

"Hey. Madison, right? Do you remember me?"

Maddy, who had not spoken to anyone socially since returning from San Francisco, was flattered but could not recall his name.

Jay sensed her hesitation. He extended his right hand.

"Jay Gordon."

Maddy blushed. "Of course I remember you."

She shook his hand anyway.

"So, how've you been?"

"Great!" Her intonation was dripping with sarcasm. "You?"

"Good. Good. Everything is good."

He was nervous but he decided to abandon the small talk.

"Hey, listen. I've seen you here a couple of times and I'm wondering if you would like to have dinner with me some night."

Maddy had not anticipated such forwardness. She also realized that Jay Gordon was the only person in the area, aside from her parents, who actually knew who she was.

"Yeah. That would be really nice," she responded without second thought.

Internally, Jay heard Queen's "We Are The Champions" serenade him as he circled the bases in a celebratory homerun trot. He managed to keep his cool.

"Great. So how might someone get in touch with you?"

"I have a cell phone. But the reception is horrible around here."

In a small filing cabinet on a shelf adjacent to where they were standing, Jay noticed a bunch of pencils and alphabetized workout cards. He pulled a random card from the file and stole a pencil from the basket.

"Sorry, Jim McKay," he said, glancing at the name on the card. "I hope you don't think any less of me."

Maddy was grinning as she recited her number.

Jay scribbled it down and tore off the corner of the card, placing it back into the file.

"So, are you in town for a while, or...?"

As soon as he asked the question, he second-guessed himself, anticipating the awkwardness of her explanation.

Maddy however, felt oddly comfortable in his presence and she abandoned her normal façade.

"To tell you truth, I don't know what I'm doing right now," she said with shy sincerity.

Jay figured he had better save the rest for the dinner table and segued into his exit speech, which he had practiced earlier in the hopes that the conversation would get this far.

"Well, I gotta run back to the restaurant, but it was good to see you. I'll call you."

As Maddy stood on the mat, a tiny smile formed on her lower lip, and Jay caught the subtle inflection before walking away. Leaving the gym, he wondered if Madison had noticed that he never even attempted to work out. He was outwardly elated and equally relieved. On the drive to Great Barrington, he cranked the *G N' R Lies* album and sang every word of every song until he pulled up in front of Porter's.

CHAPTER 23

Bucking conventional wisdom, Jay called Maddy within thirty-six hours of obtaining her number. Her phone went directly to voice mail and he left her a message.

"Hey. Madison. It's Jay Gordon, just wanted to say hello and see if you were free for dinner on Thursday night. Give me ring when you can. My home number is six-three-seven, eighty-eight hundred. And, um, I'm usually home late. Hope to talk to you soon."

Three agonizing weeks passed and Maddy never called. Not even Hugh could offer any explanation that made sense. Jay began to wonder if she had moved back to California. From their last encounter, he got the sense perhaps the degree of uncertainty caused her to distance herself from dating situations. Because of his busy schedule, Jay now only went to the gym in the early mornings, when he knew there was no chance of running into her, so he could not determine whether she was even still in the area. His disappointment slowly morphed into frustration and hostility.

He felt his ego was bruised by her inexplicable rejection. After twenty-four days, Hugh urged Jay to call her again. Reluctantly, he took his advice, and this time left her an innocuous yet slightly terse message.

"Hey, Madison. It's Jay Gordon. Give me a call whenever you get a chance." He left his home number and hung up.

Two days later, he was sitting his office at Maison going over the wine list for Porter's inaugural dinner party. The phone on his desk began ringing persistently. Normally, with two hostesses, Jay would never answer the phone during the dinner hour, but the incessant chirping was distracting enough for him to pick it up on a whim.

"Maison."

There was a pause.

"Is this Jay?"

"Speaking." His heart picked up pace.

"Hey! It's Madison Bixby."

"Oh, hey! I was beginning to wonder what happened to you."

"Me? You must be the only person alive with a phone and no answering machine. I've been calling your house for weeks."

"Oh. Sorry about that. I am a big believer in happenstance, which gives me little penchant for technology."

Maddy giggled. "That was very poetic."

All the frustration and hostility had evaporated.

"Well, let me make it up to you. Are you free this Wednesday?"

"Hmmmm," she hesitated jokingly. "I suppose."

"Great. Can I pick you up?"

"Um, how about we meet somewhere? I don't want this to feel like the prom."

Without her saying so, Jay was reminded that she was living at her parents' house.

"That's fine. Why don't you come to the restaurant? But can I still wear a corsage?"

There was an awkward silence.

"How's six-thirty?"

The other line began ringing.

"Yeah, that's perfect."

"Ah, I gotta take this call, but I'll see you then?"

"OK."

"Talk to you later."

Jay got up from his swivel chair and raised his hands above his head, signaling victory. That incessant chirping now sounded like a symphony of hummingbirds.

On Wednesday, he arranged his schedule so the workday ended in Lenox with plenty of time to shower and put on fresh clothes. He wore a navy blue Brioni blazer, pink Charvet shirt, a colorful Hermes pocket square, and his signature custom-made Barker Black shoes with the skull and crossbone logo tacked into the soles by hand. These shoes were homage to Jay's ancestor Edward Treach, the famous pirate known as Blackbeard. A light rain was falling that evening, and as he was leaving the house he opened an umbrella. Tactically, he showed up at Maison a few minutes before she arrived and unconsciously paced the perimeter of the restaurant, trying not to seem overanxious. Maddy arrived fashionably late and when he saw her car, he stepped outside to greet her with a soft hug and a gentle kiss on the cheek.

When they got in his car, Jay admitted immediately that he was "extremely nervous."

Maddy was relieved to hear this and she acknowledged that she was nervous as well. They drove to John Andrews, a nouveau American restaurant tucked in the woods of South Egremont. As they walked to their table, Jay pulled out her chair and took a moment to causally observe her outfit. Under her lightweight Burberry trench coat, which she hung carefully on an adjacent chair, she wore a sleeveless cashmere sweater, thin black dress pants tailored perfectly to fit her frame, two-inch black Mahnolo Blahnik spiked heels, and diamond-studded earrings, easily two carats apiece. Her fingers and toes were meticulously manicured and painted with a clear, glossy polish.

Over the years, Jay had cultivated his own smutty proclivity for daytime soaps and fashion magazines, so from the outset he appreciated Maddy's aesthetic. Her lips were robust, and carefully traced with a rose-tinted hue. She was quite conscious of her posture, yet not too bashful to show her well-polished teeth when she giggled. She was charismatic and articulate, and genuinely unassuming about her experiences. Throughout dinner, Jay kept thinking to himself, "God, this woman is incredible." Although she still wore her wedding ring, he noticed at times she would subconsciously cover it with her other hand when she talked about certain places she had been. Through all their discussions, not once did she directly reference any previous relationship nor did she mention the time she spent in Lenox as a teenager.

The food was exquisite. For starters, they split a bottle of Veuve Clicquot and an order of crispy fried oysters with baby greens, anchovy-mustard vinaigrette and a Parmigiano Reggiano crisp. The more they chatted and drank, the more the inherent awkwardness of a first date dissolved. By the main course, they were both giddy and ravenous, and Maddy finished her entire pan-roasted cod with clams, chorizo and saffron rice.

"I usually don't eat like this," she said as she was scraping her plate with her fork. "Actually, that's not true. What I meant to say is that I can't believe I'm eating like this."

Jay gingerly sipped his wine. "No, it's nice to see a woman with an appetite."

"You're probably thinking I'm such a heifer."

Jay burst out laughing. "Not at all. I hate going out with a woman who orders two pieces of lettuce and a bowl of steam."

Maddy rolled her eyes.

"It makes me uncomfortable. Call me crazy, but when I go out to dinner, I like to eat!" Jay lifted up his wine glass and extended it. "So, thank you for not making me feel uncomfortable."

Maddy raised her glass and clinked. "Well, thank you for not judging a girl with an appetite."

The waiter cleared their plates.

"Can I bring you anything else? Dessert? Cappuccino?" he asked with an innocent German accent.

They both looked at each other and smiled.

Jay put his palm in the air. "Madison?"

The waiter turned to her.

She sat in silence, sheepishly shaking her head.

Jay coaxed her. "C'mon, Mad." It was the first time he had abbreviated her name. It sounded strangely natural, although he wondered if it was too soon for nicknames. "Well, let's at least hear our choices."

The waiter began a tantalizing list of each dessert, how it was prepared and what it was served with. When he was finished, Maddy's expression had not changed.

"Nothing for me, thank you."

Jay turned to the waiter. "I'll have a decaf and the check, please."

"Very well." The waiter seemed disappointed he couldn't sell a dessert after his lengthy descriptions.

Before Jay could ask, Maddy explained herself. "I don't have much of a sweet tooth. I mean, those deserts sound amazing, but—"

"It's fine," Jay said. "I'm not in the mood for the homemade caramel ice cream with the ginger crème brulée anyway."

When they got back to Lenox, Jay got out of the car first and opened the passenger side door. This was something Fritz would do, and she found it touching and thoughtful. Their goodbye hug lasted a comfortable forty-five seconds and then he kissed her deliberately on her inner cheek and patted the back of her coat gracefully. A light drizzle was falling under the parking lot light, and a sparkly mist blanketed the outer layer of her hair. Before getting back into his car, Jay looked eagerly into her eyes.

"I had a really nice time tonight."

"I did too." Her voice was timid and earnest.

"I'll call you."

"You need to get an answering machine, or a cell phone!" she said, half in jest.

"I told you, I don't believe in technology. I believe in—"

"Happenstance." Maddy finished his sentence. "I know. It's very endearing."

Jay slipped into his car and quickly powered down his window. "Drive safe."

She waved. Before leaving the parking lot, she took a deep breath and examined herself in the rearview mirror.

Maddy returned to her loft above the carport in her parent's garage. The space was still full of old boxes and rusty tools. It smelled like mothballs and motor oil, but she had organized her sleeping area so it was at least comfortable and clean. Her suitcases were neatly arranged on the floor and lying open as if each were its own dresser. A thin, wooden beam hovered above the foot of her bed and she hung various articles of clothes on coat hangers. Down a creaky, banister-less flight of steps, the bathroom was a small closet with a paint-spattered sink and a single stall shower. The mirror was scratched and faded, making it difficult for her to "fix her face." One might imagine such a drastic change of lifestyle would trigger another spell of depression. This was not the case. As she tucked herself into bed that night, she felt a new sense of tranquility and optimism.

Since returning to Lenox, she managed to resurrect some semblance of a relationship with her family. On one occasion, Jackie and Johnny both came home and the Horns had dinner in the dining room for the first time in nearly fifteen years. Although everyone assumed her marriage was defunct, she never spoke of *why* she had come home. Out of respect for her parents' traditional values, she continued wearing her wedding ring, which also allowed her to feel benignly Christian while encouraging speculation about her situation. Naturally, she went through periods of gloominess, but overall she was happy to be independent and, at least temporarily, single.

CHAPTER 24

While Jay sleeps in the passenger seat, Smitty gingerly depresses the gas pedal of the Range Rover. It is two PM and they have just begun the long westward haul on Interstate 16. Craving a greasy spoon breakfast, Smitty is reluctant to wake his counterpart prematurely. Axl, slightly dehydrated from the air conditioning, pants rhythmically from the back. Smitty scans the AM dial until he finds Jim Rome on the Atlanta sports radio affiliate, WCNN-680. The droning dissection of Pac Ten football and Angelina Jolie's penchant for third world children does not bother Jay, who has been immodestly snoring through his nostrils. But as Rome returns from a commercial break, Smitty raises the volume on the show's signature theme song. The intro to Guns N' Roses' "Welcome to the Jungle" rings out and Jay opens his eyes.

"There he is, folks!" Smitty is now famished.

"Where the hell are we?"

"We're east of Atlanta."

Jay seems disoriented. "Yeah? Did you follow your li'l map, you li'l bitch?"

Smitty exhales defensively.

"It's your map. How 'bout some fucking Waffle House, big guy?"

Jay rubs his eyes. "Is this my Appetite CD?" he says while yawning.

Smitty shakes his head.

Jay sits up in his seat, cranks the stereo and turns to the back. "You hear that, Axl? This is our jam, buddy!" Axl is still panting and begins licking Jay's hand.

"Did you say Waffle House?" Jay is suddenly giddy.

"Did you say appetite?" Smitty is single-minded. "I could really fuck up some waffles and syrup right about now."

"Surrrup," Jay responds with a Dixieland inflection.

"Surrrup," Smitty echoes back.

Jay lowers the volume of the radio as Rome's irreverent voice eclipses the song. "So what's the game plan, Clyde?"

Smitty chuckles under his breath. It has been a long time since anyone has called him Clyde. The nickname came from his aversion to people referring to him as Walter, or even Walt. At boarding school, his closest friends gave him the Clyde moniker after New York Knicks great Walt "Clyde" Frazier. Much to his chagrin, the name stuck for a full semester, but later became more of a term of endearment than an adolescent temper tester. After college, anyone who still called Smitty "Clyde" did it in fond nostalgia.

"Boom! There we fucking go! I love the South!" Smitty veers to the right as he spots the yellow block letters of Waffle House from a tall signpost in the distance. At the same time, a purple Dodge Neon with racing stripes and an aerodynamic rear grill comes barreling down the highway, almost obstructing the turning lane. Jay resolutely cautions Smitty's progress. "Yo! Watch out for Dale Jr. over here on the right."

"I see him." Smitty continues into his turn, impeding the progress of the oncoming car. The driver, a freckly teenager wearing a big-fit red T-shirt and a dog collar necklace, blares his horn and swerves into the left lane. He speeds up next to the Range Rover and flips up his middle finger. Smitty plays along, gesticulating oral sex by wiggling his tongue inside his mouth.

"Oh jeezus," Jay murmurs halfheartedly. "Don't incite this nut."

The teenager lays his hand on the horn and sticks up his middle finger again, slowly mouthing the word, "Ass-hole!"

"Fuck this slack-jawed yokel." Smitty is

amused but quickly dips to the right so he will not miss his exit.

The Waffle House is an incomparable haven for cheap southern grub and sweaty hospitality. Well satiated by sweet batter and comforting grease, Jay leaves the diner with a Styrofoam platter full of steak and eggs for Axl.

"Here you go, king basset." Axl is literally drooling.

Smitty emerges outside sipping on a to-go cup of iced sweet tea.

Jay puckers his lips. "I don't how you can drink that shit in this heat. Just makes you more thirsty."

In the parking lot, the early fall humidity is oppressive as the hazy sun is captured by the freshly paved blacktop. Jay fills Axl's water dish with a bottle of Dasani that has been sitting in the backseat for the duration of the trip. Smitty pulls out the map again, almost inciting some sort of mockery. Jay refrains.

"If we cut through Georgia on highway ninety-six, I think we can make it to Nashville, Tennessee by nightfall."

Jay bobs his head methodically. "I'm just getting tired as shit, dude. I gotta do some work, figure some things out businesswise."

Smitty continues to study the map. "So

what do you want to do, boss? It's too hot to play golf and we still have a lot of road to cover."

An air of diplomacy has returned to their dialogue.

"I don't know. Let's just keep driving, but can we agree on at least four stars wherever we stop tonight?"

Smitty stretches his arms. "I'm with you on that."

Axl furiously gobbles his breakfast and slurps the warm water from his dish. When he is finished, he leaps back into his seat and the three travelers resume their voyage.

CHAPTER 25

The night after dinner at John Andrews, Maddy received a message from Jay, thanking her for a lovely evening. When she called him back, his phone rang and rang but he was not home. The next morning she showed up at Lenox Fitness Center before nine AM, hoping to run into him. As she inched up the driveway, she spotted his S4 parked near the side entrance. She felt a smile overtake her mouth and she fixed her hair and reapplied lip gloss. As she checked in, Jay was just exiting the lobby heading home to shower. He was not expecting to see Madison at the gym so early and had not applied deodorant before leaving the locker room.

"Hey you!" she said gleefully.

"Hey." Jay was sweaty and self-conscious of his odor. They embraced awkwardly yet affectionately.

"You're an early bird."

Jay glanced at the clock on the wall, which read 9:05. He had been up since 5:45.

"Just tryin' to get that worm."

Maddy giggled. "Did you get it?"

"Not yet, but it's still early," Jay replied. "I'm late for a meeting, but gimme a shout later."

"OK, Jay Gordon."

"Enjoy your workout." As Jay left the building, he sniffed his armpit and detected a slight musky funk.

"Fuck," he mouthed to himself.

Later that afternoon, Maddy took a trip to Pittsfield and bought Jay the latest Motorola flip phone from a kiosk at the Berkshire Mall. She had it gift wrapped and she personalized the greeting card, which read:

Dear Jay,
With this, I hope you discover
that the intersection of technol-
ogy and happenstance is really a
happy place.
Enjoy!
Madison

She addressed it to Jay Gordon c/o Maison and sent it to the restaurant from the post office in downtown Lenox.

Jay received the package the next day. He

cut the box open with a Swiss Army knife and the card fell to the floor. Jay read it three times consecutively and then sat down at his desk. He paused for a second and then grabbed the office phone and dialed Maddy's number, which he had already committed to memory. She was sitting outside at Lenox Coffee Roasters sipping a smoothie, flipping through pages of *In Style*.

"Hello, Jay." She recognized the number from the caller ID.

"You'll never believe what I did today."

Maddy grinned. "Oh, do tell."

"I entered the twenty-first century. I surrendered to the technology revolution."

"You surrendered? Not under duress I hope."

"No, no. Au contraire, this *really* beautiful, thoughtful girl gave me a communications makeover."

"Wow."

Jay interrupted, not wanting to overdo the charade. "Anyway, thank you so much!"

"My pleasure."

"What are you doing right now? I want to see you."

"Oh, I'm really busy." Maddy tried to sound serious but was smiling. "I'm reading fashion mags and drinking a Jazzy Jamaican."

"The Reggae Raspberry is waay better."

"Au contraire!"

"Well, that does sound hectic." Jay tried to sound serious but *he* was smiling. "Maybe I'll try you at a better time?"

"No. Come here. I want to *see* you!"

"I'll be there in a half-hour."

The sun was setting when he pulled into the parking lot of the coffee shop. The large smoothie cup in her hand was empty, but Maddy was still perched on the porch in her oversized shades. She waved to Jay with one finger as he got out of his car and skipped up the steps. He kissed her on the cheek, an inch from her lips.

"I know it's kinda early, but I hope you're hungry, 'cause I have a plan for dinner."

"I *am* a little hungry! I'm really tired though. Do you mind if I get a coffee before we go."

"No, that actually sounds good. I could use a little caffeine too."

She ordered a double-shot dry cappuccino with skim milk and Jay got a regular latte to go. Maddy insisted on paying.

Their second date was as distinct and magnificent as the first. They drove to Williamstown, thirty minutes north of Lenox, and ate a specially prepared, off the menu feast at Spundiggers Barbecue, a soul food restaurant owned by Jay's buddy Clayton. Afterwards, they went to see a seven-piece jazz band at the Copper Coin, a local club on Union Street. In between sets, they took a stroll on the cobblestone sidewalk. Maddy hooked her arm around his elbow, lightly touching his bicep with her fingertips. A few steps later, Jay slowly turned and pulled Maddy close to him so her cheek brushed against his delicate scruff. Under the soft glow of the streetlight, they shared a long, passionate kiss.

The progression of their romance elevated with each encounter. Jay invited Maddy to his house and cooked his specialty: seared ahi tuna with braised bok choy and crispy shrimp spring rolls. Afterwards, they sat outside on the back deck and finished off the evening's third bottle of Rudd Chardonnay.

They chatted about places they had traveled to and experiences they shared in common, such as eating the Oysters and Pearls at The French Laundry in Napa, and surviving the Tower of Terror at Disney World in Orlando. They discovered that they were both devotees of *Melrose Place* and, more recently, *Sex in the City*, and Jay and Maddy dissected each character and relationship with the thorough precision of NFL analysts on a pre-game show. They talked and laughed well into the night and although Jay was trying to make an impression, he grew increasingly comfortable and confident in her presence. Madison still wore a wedding ring, which, for the moment, Jay made a conscious effort not to mention or even glance at, yet given the context of how they initially met, it was becoming the proverbial elephant in the room.

Jay's house was set back from the road and secluded by a cluster of pine trees and a tiny brook that dried up during the late summer months. It was a three-story colonial with a wraparound back deck and a half-circle gravel driveway. His bedroom was distinctly Californian. His dressers and matching end tables were crafted from Humboldt county mock Redwood, and the clothes and shoes were neatly organized in a California closet. His bed was a California king and the paintings on the walls were wood-framed oil-based landscapes of vineyards in Sonoma County. The rest of the house was indicative of a fully furnished rental, except for the living room, where Jay replaced the seating with his own beige L-shaped Italian leather coach and a glass coffee table overflowing with coasters from his personal collection.

Maddy got up from the deck to use the bathroom, whisking open the sliding door. After she was out of sight, Jay slipped inside and pretended to rearrange the magazines on the bookshelf underneath the gooseneck lamp. When she emerged, he pounced on her and tackled her playfully. They fell onto the couch and a session of heated foreplay ensued. As Jay was unbuttoning her jeans, she held up her hand, flexing her ring finger.

"I can't."

Jay held his breath.

"I'm... married."

Maddy sat up. For several minutes she kept her head bent toward her lap and did not speak. Jay waited patiently but ran his fingers through his hair, tightly gripping the locks on the top of his head out of frustration. Finally she looked up.

"Are you free tomorrow evening?"

Jay was somewhat startled.

"Uh, yeah. I can be. Do you want to do something?"

In the context of the situation, his control had just seeped through a sieve.

"I need to go now. But call me tomorrow, OK?" With an air of nonchalance, Maddy got up from the couch and leaned down to kiss Jay on the cheek. Then she grabbed her bag and car keys from the hallway chest and scurried out the front door. Jay remained seated on the couch, scratching his scruff. He was frustrated with himself for not bringing up the subject of her marriage on his terms.

Madison awoke early the next morning. After brushing her teeth, she slid off her wedding ring and set it in a box next to her bed. She drove immediately to the spa at Canyon Ranch for a bikini wax. Then she made dinner reservations at for two at Roma, a Northern Italian trattoria located on Railroad Street, directly across from Porter's.

All day Jay debated whether or not to call her. During meetings about Porter's impending launch party, his mind kept drifting back to that moment on the couch. Finally, around four PM, he dialed Maddy from the office phone. Madison answered in an unusually cheery voice. After exchanging mildly awkward pleasantries, she told him about their dinner reservations at Roma. From this exchange, it was clear that Maddy was "the dealer" and Jay had become an anxious patron at the blackjack table, waiting to be dealt his hand. He agreed to meet her, but resolved to show up late. As the dinner hour approached, he sat upstairs in the office, waiting for Maddy's car. From his window, he could see down the one-way street and into the front entrance of Roma. Maddy appeared at sunset in her burgundy drop top. Jay felt his palms clam up. She looked radiant and he noticed the late shoppers and pedestrians on

Railroad Street all turn and gawk as she parallel parked. He managed to wait only a few minutes before going out to meet her. As he stepped through the entrance, Maddy was at the first table, waiting with an opened bottle of Barolo. Jay noticed immediately that she was not wearing her ring.

"Hey, how *are* you? How was your day?" She did not stand up to greet him, so Jay removed his blazer and sat down. He poured himself a glass of wine before answering.

"It was busy."

Jay's mind began racing again. He was hoping for instant contrition and a straightforward explanation, but instead Maddy began a casual dissertation on how shopping in the Berkshires was so "insipid" compared to New York City and London. Inside the restaurant, an early dinner buzz drowned out some of Maddy's vibrant intonations. Jay sat there patiently, swirling his wine glass and observing her practiced smile and delicate, polished fingers gesticulate as she named stores and referenced chic urban hubs. Finally, he turned his head; making it obvious he was no longer listening.

"Jay?"

"Can we talk about the fact that *you're married*!"

Maddy's lighthearted expression turned.

It was as if those little words were sharp pins, puncturing and deflating her demeanor. She could not remember the last time she was asked to candidly confront something she was deliberately avoiding. She froze, staring down at her empty ring finger. Jay took a sip of his wine, relieved he was able to finally steer the direction of their conversation.

The fusion of dinner conversations from the surrounding tables was amplified and as Maddy stared emptily into the breadbasket her silence announced her vulnerability. When she looked up at Jay, she noticed his eyes had shifted from her. Every familiar instinct urged her to get up from the table and walk away. Her hands grew clammy and her neck perspired. After what felt an hour, Jay calmly tapped his palm on the table, lifted his napkin off his lap and slid his chair back.

"I'm gonna go use the restr—"

Maddy reached across the table and clasped his hand.

"No. Wait."

The tone of her voice wavered with vacillation. She began by pointing to her empty ring finger. Using unspecific language, she explained how her relationship with Julian had deteriorated quickly and how her loyalty was not to the man she married but to her family, who disapproved of divorce. This was somewhat of a claptrap clarification and with all the other unspoken variables—her affair with Fritz, her first marriage to Jed, her inability to even talk to her family, her lack of direction in life—she spoke with little conviction. The conversation lasted throughout dinner and Maddy barely touched her linguini and clams. She was terrified that exposing some of her personal baggage would give Jay a reason to distance himself from her. Jay ate his eggplant parmigiana, sipped his wine and quietly listened, sensing her hesitation and uncertainty.

After dinner, Jay offered Maddy his hand and he guided her out of the restaurant with consolatory assertiveness. He walked her to her car and before she got in, he beckoned her to his arms.

"C'mere."

Maddy smiled, and her eyes glistened from the tears that formed but never tumbled. She sighed deeply as she pressed her cheek against his chest. He hugged her with a reassuring firmness and kissed her on her forehead.

Maddy followed Jay back to his house. When they got inside, Jay opened another bottle of Barolo from his personal collection. The atmosphere felt heavy, so to deemphasize the evening's subject matter, he dusted off his

Eddie Murphy: Delirious DVD, hoping that classic comedy as background noise would lighten the mood.

It worked. They chatted casually, laughed heartily and drank several glasses of wine. Maddy regained her appetite and ate most of the food from her doggy bag. When the movie ended, they were in a cuddle position on the couch. Jay was stroking her hair and he asked cautiously if she would like to spend the night. Madison nodded with no hesitation, and for the first time that night Jay felt a surge of sexual tension. He led her up the stairs, but before they reached the top, Maddy grabbed him. They paused, and the sound of their conjoining lips was passionately visceral. Moments later they were in his bedroom disrobing each other frantically. Having tended to her bikini line earlier that morning, Maddy was unrestrained.

Without the assistance of an alarm clock, Jay woke up early, as usual. His physical frame ached from excessive wine consumption and primal overindulgence. Madison was sleeping naked under the sheets. A chilly morning breeze fluttered the thin drapes by the bureau, and as Jay slipped out of bed he shut the window so the draft would not wake her. Since Porter's inaugural party was only two days away, his first destination that morning was Great Barrington. This meant he would not return home until the kitchen closed at Maison later that evening. After showering, he wrote Maddy a quick note.

Dear Princess,
I am off to work. Busy day again.
Let yourself out whenever you
want. The door will lock behind
you. I'll call you later. (From my
cell phone!)
~ Sunshine

Jay tried calling her at various points throughout the day but her phone was turned off. Not hearing from her gave him a sinking feeling that something had gone wrong or perhaps she was having second thoughts. Again his mind wandered, contemplating hypothetical scenarios. By nightfall he was back in Lenox, and after eating a brief dinner at Maison he headed home. As he pulled into his driveway, he noticed Maddy's car had not moved since the night before. He had thought about her incessantly all day, and at various times he was so detached from his work he needed to take walks around the block to get his head back in the game. Although he was ravenously attracted to her, he was equally intrigued by the idea of Maddy—her sophisticated personality, her cosmopolitan sensibility and her glamorous proclivities. Her "type" was an anomaly in the Berkshires, and after the events of the previous two nights, he was concerned that perhaps he had prematurely forced a full-fledged dialogue in the relationship.

When he stepped inside, she greeted him with a soft squeeze and an open-mouth kiss. It felt good to have her waiting when he got home, and her presence reassured him that she was not having second thoughts. She was dressed entirely in clothes plucked from his closet: an old gray T-shirt, a pair of Jay's custom-made white boxers and a terrycloth Frette bathrobe with "JG" embroidered on the front. As they embraced, he began smoothing her inner legs with his palms and she unabashedly massaged between his legs. Hastily, he tossed his blazer toward the coat-rack and lifted her off her feet, carrying her to the couch. A glass vase that sat innocently on the end table was kicked to the floor in a cyclone of lustful fervor. The loud shattering only enhanced the raw energy.

Jay woke up to the sound of the grandfather clock in the hallway ringing twice. He shook Maddy, who was sprawled precariously across the back pillows of the couch. She was difficult to wake, but eventually she rose with a disheveled yawn. The lights downstairs were still on, and the feeling of electric grogginess pervaded the house. Maddy scurried upstairs, warily avoiding the glass fragments scattered across the dark cherry hardwood. Jay shut off the lights and joined her in bed. The sheets were cool for a minute, then comfortingly warm as the king size bed enveloped two tired bodies.

Madison woke up around nine-thirty the next morning. Jay was gone. No note this time. She had a subconscious recollection of him hurrying around as if he was late for something. Crablike, she grabbed at the bedside table until she located the DirecTV remote. She snapped on the small LCD set that hung on a wall mount above Jay's dresser and scanned the channels until she landed on *Live! With Regis & Kelly*. The perky voice of Kelly Ripa accompanied by occasional laughs and cheers from the studio audience muffled the intermittent chirping of birds outside the window. It had been some time since Maddy had spent consecutive mornings surrounded by creature comforts and she was in no hurry to leave. Soon, she drifted back to sleep.

A venomous argument between Victor and Nikki caused Maddy to stir. She blinked a few times and sat up in bed, realizing that her innocuous dream had just melded with a recent plot of *The Young and the Restless,* which was now blaring from the television. The alarm clock read 2:07 PM. With a forceful thrust, she hopped on to her feet, still clenching the sheets like a cat reaching to sharpen its claws on a scratching post. She stretched, and noticed that her T-shirt was torn at the collar. After a long shower and a quick snoop around Jay's bathroom, she put on her own clothes and found her car keys, making her way downstairs. As she stepped outside, the front door latched behind her and the afternoon sun felt harsh on her eyes.

CHAPTER 26

"Lemme get this straight…"

Night has fallen and Smitty has been driving all day.

"…This chick spends two days and two nights at your house. Sleeps in. Borrows your clothes. Eats your food—"

"Presumably," Jay interjects.

"OK. Presumably. But you said her car never moved."

"Yeah. I *presume* she helped herself to food while I was gone for fourteen hours."

"I think that's a fair presumption." Smitty pauses to process everything. "So basically, you sleep with her once and she moves in."

Jay is beaming. "Basically. Yeah, was a bit odd, but I kind of liked it. I was really digging this chick. I wanted her to be there. But you know what's fucked up?"

Smitty has one hand on the wheel. His

other elbow is leaning on the window. "The whole thing is fucked up, Jay."

"You know that glass vase we broke?"

"Yeah."

"She just left it smashed on the floor. I came home that night and cut my foot because I forgot it was there." Jay scratches his chin introspectively. "I never told her about that."

"You cut your foot"

Smitty chuckles out of pity.

"I don't know about this girl, dude. She just left you with a room full of broken glass?"

"At the time, it wasn't a big deal. I would've swept it up in the morning except I was late. And you know me, Smit. I am *never* late to *anything*, and that morning I missed half of a meeting because I couldn't wake up."

Jay pauses and the tinge of anger in his voice dissipates.

"You know what, though? The sex made it all worthwhile. That girl wore me out. She was a fucking wild animal. Or, I should say, a wild fucking animal."

Smitty looks on incredulously.

"Anyway, those first few weeks were incredible. Best sex of my life, by a country mile."

Smitty shakes his head. "I can see where this is going. For your sake, I wish the sex had been stale so you had nothing to cling to when everything got ugly."

"With all due respect, Clyde, you have no idea where this is going."

Smitty changes the subject. "There you go, Jaybo!" He elbows him and points to the right. Off the highway, in the distance, there is a massive indoor/outdoor sports facility flagged by an equally immense neon facade that reads: **Jasper County Pitch 'N' Put— Open 24 Hours**.

"You still wanna play golf?"

"Don't be a cock."

"What? Mini golf is awesome."

"Yeah, if you're on 'shrooms."

"That's a great idea! Let's get some mush-ies!"

"You're out of line."

"No, really. I could use a good mind fuck."

Jay exaggeratedly exhales. "That's the last thing we need right now."

Smitty snaps open his seat belt buckle, loosening his mobility. "Either way, I'm fixin' to get banged up tonight. How much Demerol do we have left?"

"Plenty. We haven't smoked all day either."

"That's a good thing. Smoking greenery with blue state plates in the deep South—

you're just asking for a cop to pistol-whip you."

"Alright, Smitty."

"Plus, this is bulldog country and we're traveling with a basset hound."

"OK. I get it."

"You know, folks down here think the Civil War is at halftime."

Jay starts singing the *Dukes of Hazzard* theme song. *"They're just some good ole boys, never meanin' no harm, beats all you ever saw, been in trouble with the law since the day they were born."*

Smitty chimes in, mumbling the lyrics incoherently. *"Straightenin' the curves, flattenin' the hill, someday the mountain may get them but the law never will."*

Jay affectionately pounds the armrest with his fist. "The General Lee ain't got shit on this beast! Three hundred horses, Smitty. Three hundred horses and not a fucking sound!"

Smitty nods. "I had her in a full gallop earlier. She did pretty well."

"Fuckin' right!"

Smitty conjures an aphorism. "You can speed but you can't smoke weed."

"Yeah, that's great Smit. Hey, listen. I'm afraid that five-star hotel plan may be tricky tonight."

Smitty puckers his lips. "I'm thinking the same thing."

"So, how 'bout when we get to Nashville, we find a Marriott and get drunk."

"Perfect."

CHAPTER 27

Maddy was what Hugh referred to as a total head turner. She could work a crowd with the proficiency of Wall Street power broker. In social situations, Jay relished her company. With the early success of Maison, he became increasingly conscious of the way he was perceived by the local community, and he believed Madison boosted his image. On the evening of Porter's launch party, they split a bottle of 2002 Sine Qua Non Hollerin' M Pinot Noir and each ate a Vicodin while they were getting ready. She wore a Roberto Cavalli dress with some spiky Jimmy Choo's and her Graff diamond earrings.

When they pulled up to the valet at the top of Railroad Street, Jay got out first and walked around to open the passenger side door. Maddy took his hand and pulled herself up, tilting her head back so her perfectly brushed hair cascaded in place. It was a cloudy, humid evening and the threat of rain rumbled from above. Undeterred by the murky skies, a swarm of well-dressed revelers stood sipping drinks inside a roped-off section of the sidewalk. Maddy walked a step ahead of Jay, who kept his hand on her waist as they meandered through the crowd and up to the bar. Earlier she had stated, in no uncertain terms, that she would only drink Sapphire and tonics.

"Why only gin tonight?" Jay asked innocently.

"Because anything other than a colorless drink will clash with what I am wearing." Jay secretly admired her obsessive sense of social apropos.

At the bar, he ordered himself a Lagavulin with a splash of soda and a Sapphire and tonic. During mingling hour, Jay was pulled aside by the wife of one of his business partners. Gazing at Maddy, she whispered, "Where'd you find *her*?"

§   §   §

After a few weeks, Maddy was fully moved in.

She transported her wardrobe in increments and Jay cleared out the adjacent closet in the master bedroom. She spent most days hanging around the house watching TV, reading magazines or shooting pellet guns off the back deck. In a locked cabinet in the downstairs study, she had discovered Jay's antique gun collection.

The night of July 4th, 2003, they packed a bottle of Dom Perignon and a picnic blanket, and drove to Stockbridge Bowl to watch the fireworks. When they returned home, Maddy lured Jay into the downstairs study. For Maddy, long rifles were archetypal Freudian eroticism, and as Jay lubricated the barrel of his Holland and Holland 12-bore royal shotgun, she dropped to her knees and forced him into her mouth. Minutes later, they had aggressive sex on the carpet, and afterwards Jay massaged Neosporin on her bare backside to calm the rug burn.

Before falling asleep that night, Madison grew quiet and detached. Jay had never seen this side of her. They lay in bed with the lights on, but she would not turn toward him. He tried putting his arms around her and she shrugged him off. He attempted to verbally console her, but she would not respond. Finally, he turned off the lights and rolled over to his side of the bed.

"This is not about you," she said, breaking her ninety-minute silence.

Jay was agitated. "Well, what the fuck, Madison? What am I supposed to think?"

He waited for her response. Through the bedroom window, a symphony of crickets filled the pause.

"Every Fourth of July, I think something bad is about to happen."

Maddy's voice was low and quivery. "I get this feeling that everyone will leave and I will be left alone."

Jay slid next to her and began rubbing her back softly. Her eyes became teary and a lump formed in her throat. After another long pause, she cautiously explained some of her experiences at Faith First, culminating with the Fourth of July barbecue.

"I've never spoken about this to anyone."

Jay kept moving his palm on her back at a reassuring pace, but he did not know how to respond. The evening had spanned a full spectrum of emotions and he was mentally exhausted. In a moment of gracious humility, Maddy turned toward Jay and wrapped her arms and legs around him, pressing her moistened cheek against the stubble on his neck.

"Don't ever leave me," she whispered.

"It's OK, Mad, I'm right here."

CHAPTER 28

Over time, Jay gradually learned about Maddy's previous relationships and the details of her pending divorce. Speaking openly was not something that came naturally to Madison Horn, so a cloud of static often hovered over their interactions.

As Jay's work schedule settled, Maddy surprised him with two tickets to Miami Beach. She paid for their four-night stay at the Hotel Elando. It was their first vacation as a couple, and on the flight to Florida, Jay joined the mile high club. Maddy would not disclose whether or not she was already a member. From the moment they boarded the flight in Hartford, the trip became an inebriated binge. The time away was ideal for Jay, who had lately been so preoccupied with his restaurants, he had found little time to revisit old party habits. Several rum and cokes were consumed at high altitudes, which made for a sloppy arrival at Miami International Airport. Jay had packed a bottle of Patron, which they opened on the cab ride to the hotel.

In the sweltering humidity, Jay was in rare form, handing out twenty-dollar tips to the bellhops and playfully groping Maddy in conspicuous places. They walked down Lincoln Road hand in hand, stopping at Nexxt Café for an early outdoor dinner. When they returned to the Elando, Maddy went upstairs to change into her bikini. Jay, who was wearing his bathing suit underneath his shorts, waited at the bar. Having attracted particular attention from his earlier generosity, he was approached by the head concierge.

"Mr. Gordon. Hullo." The man, presumably a Cuban immigrant, spoke in a suave tone. He extended his hand gregariously.

"Esteban."

Jay was still tipsy and he clasped the man's hand between both palms.

"How you doing. Jay Gordon."

"Ah, very well, thank jou. Is everything to jou liking so far?"

Jay was overrun by a glazed, jovial stare.

"Everything is wonderful."

"Is there anything we can do for jou, sir?"

Jay beckoned for the man to come closer.

"How can I get some California Corn-flakes?"

"Essscuzme? I don't know this."

"You know." He sniffed laterally across his finger.

"Ah, jess. Cocann. No problem."

"Really?"

"For jou? No problem."

Maddy emerged from the elevator wearing a sun hat and a thin beach skirt. Jay put his finger over his lips and patted the man on the shoulder.

"See you in a while."

He lifted Maddy up and carried her out of the hotel and onto the street. It was an ideal time of day for a swim. The evening sky was pigmented like pomegranate seeds had been dragged across the westward horizon. They set up a large quilt on the soft sand. Maddy wanted to touch the water right away, but Jay was content relaxing on the shore in the glow of the late-day sun. When his daylong buzz began to wane, he gathered Maddy and they headed back to the hotel. The concierge met them in their lobby.

"Yo! Esteban!"

He smiled courteously at Madison and handed Jay a Romeo y Julieta case, which seemed unusually light. Esteban was careful with his words.

"Esa good ceegar. Very strong."

Jay was somewhat surprised. "Oh, that's great! Thank you, my friend!"

In the elevator he decided to tell Maddy.

"Do you know what this is?" Beaming, he tapped the cigar case.

Maddy was somewhat suspicious. "It's not a cigar?"

Jay shook his head.

"What then?"

"Cali Cornflakes," he said sheepishly.

Maddy looked puzzled. "What is *that*, meth?"

"Meth? What? No. You think I'm a fucking junkie?"

Maddy played the indignant diva. "Well, I don't fucking know, Jay. You and our little friend down there were acting sketchy."

"Sketchy? That's Esteban! He's a manager at one of the nicest hotels in Miami. You're just jealous he didn't bring *you* a party favor."

Before the elevator door closed, an elderly European couple walked in. The husband was dripping wet, wearing flip-flops and a tight purple Speedo, a Budweiser towel draped around his shoulders. Jay quickly glanced at Maddy, who was smiling in disbelief.

He mustered his most serious face. "Uh, what floor?"

"Fumpf. Danke."

The wife was heavyset, wearing a long, white robe with the Elando logo embroidered on the front pocket. "Ja," she said, pointing to the control pad.

Jay looked at Maddy again. She was holding up five fingers.

He pushed the button. A humorously tense stillness ensued. Jay knew that if he looked at Maddy, he would lose his composure.

Walking into the hotel room, Jay took the cigar case and teasingly poked her between her butt cheeks. She jumped up startled, slapping his hand. Jay was giggling and he tackled her on the bed in an uncompetitive headlock. Wrestling turned into foreplay, but just before they had sex, Jay opened the Romeo y Julieta and crushed up two "bumps." Madison had never done hard drugs, and the feeling of sin only enhanced the levels of intimacy.

§   §   §

The trip to Miami solidified their desire to be with one another.

"Crazy in love," is what Jay would say to Hugh when he asked how he was doing.

Maddy reunited with Rachel Rothstein and periodically drove to Manhattan for a midweek sojourn. On the ride back, she would

meander through southern Connecticut looking for a place to have lunch. One afternoon,
next to a quaint café on Fullerton Street, she
stumbled upon a boutique gun shop in downtown Darien. In the window stood an authen-
tic Civil War rifle with a $4,500 price tag.
Financially, the gun represented more than
two weeks of Julian's monthly allowance, but
she wanted something special for Jay's birthday. She paid with her debit card. The man
gift wrapped the rifle in an elegant box with
a sketched engraving of Robert E. Lee in the
corner above the store logo.

Maddy got home after dark that night
and set the box on the bed. She changed into
her La Perla lingerie and a left a bottle of
champagne chilling on the dresser.

When Jay returned from work, he was
astounded by the gift and equally touched by
Maddy's thorough and thoughtful presenta-
tion.

Sex that night was prolonged and passionate, and afterwards they lay in bed eating ice
cream and chatting.

"I need to go to San Francisco at some
point for a deposition. I'm not sure when,
but it should be sometime in the next six
months. Would you come with me?" Maddy
asked sheepishly. "It's for this whole divorce
thing."

Jay was both flattered and stunned, as Maddy never made unsolicited conversation regarding her failed marriage. He kissed her on her forehead. "Of course I will go with you. I'm happy you asked." He winked at her teasingly. "And thank you for providing me with a little advance notice."

Out of sheer curiosity, Jay started prying tidbits of information from Maddy about her divorce settlement. Then, over the next month, he pieced together his own hypothesis. He remembered a conversation they'd had at dinner one night when Maddy flippantly mentioned that through her work at Dobson & Verlander she could estimate Julian's net worth somewhere around forty or fifty million. Jay speculated, with the proliferation of private equity deals since that time, he could have easily doubled his fortune. Although Madison repeatedly indicated that she was only seeking a reasonable settlement, Jay believed that she was naïve about how much money was potentially at stake. As he contemplated the possibilities, it became difficult for him to remain benignly objective about his feelings for her. He just kept thinking to himself: "This is too good to be true."

Their relationship had progressed so quickly, it felt natural for him to at least entertain the possibility of settling down.

There were those times when Maddy was cold and despondent, and Jay had learned to embrace such mood swings with affection. He was enamored by her charisma and somehow found her multifaceted quirkiness endearing. The next night, after dinner at Maison, they walked around the block with their hands tightly clasped. A slow procession of clouds covered the crescent moon, leaving the streets dimly illuminated.

"I've never felt like this with anyone," Jay professed. "You're just amazing, in so many ways." He kissed two of his fingers and delicately placed them on her lips.

"You know—" Maddy paused as a lump formed in her throat. "You're the only person who has ever taken the time to get to know me."

Her eyes glistened.

Jay kissed her again. "I can't imagine anyone not wanting to get to know you."

Maddy blinked and two tiny tears trickled down her cheeks. Jay blotted the moisture on her face with the side of his index finger. They walked in silence for a while, passing the penny candy store on Church Street and circling back to the parking lot at Maison.

§   §   §

Jay Gordon and Madison Horn emerged as Lenox's version of a power couple. With the absence of tabloid headlines, small town socialites vicariously followed their romance through a whispering word of mouth. The Horn family, however, was unaware that Jay was anything more than a friend. Maddy told her traditionally minded family that she was renting a house from Jay, who lived in Stockbridge with his girlfriend. When Jane and Bill came for a visit, Maddy carefully removed all the pictures of Jay and his family from the walls and bookshelves. She replaced the men's magazines with *Glamour, Tatler* and *Cosmopolitan.* Jay was conflicted because it did not seem ethical to deceive his girlfriend's parents, but Maddy kept saying, "You don't understand my family." Jay reluctantly went along, but insisted after the divorce was finalized that they come clean.

Since Porter's and Maison were open for both lunch and dinner seven days a week in the summer months, essentially every day was a workday. The only time Jay was not working was when he left the area. Each morning began the same way. He woke up early, prepared coffee for Maddy and headed to Maison to cash out from the night before. Maddy would get to the restaurant around ten-thirty and Jay would cook her the same breakfast:

two poached eggs, dry wheat toast and half a grapefruit. Then they would go to the gym and work out with a personal trainer before parting ways for a few hours while Jay drove to Great Barrington to check on Porter's. Maddy would call frequently, asking when he was coming home and constantly telling him that she missed him.

They became as inseparable as was possible. Toward the end of the summer, weekdays were less hectic in the restaurant business and Jay took full advantage. They chartered private planes to Nantucket and hired car services for quick trips to New York and Boston. They lodged in luxury cottages and chic urban hotels and ate at world-renowned restaurants.

Maddy regained her shopping impetus and began spending money as if she had already received her settlement. This concerned Jay, but as someone with his own proclivities for lavish indulgences, he bit his tongue.

Later that fall, Maddy decided to volunteer at an animal farm two mornings a week. She attributed this inspiration to Jay, and believed that physical labor and affection for animals would help de-emphasize her material self-involvement. It was the first time Maddy had worked since leaving Jed and she was diligent about her hours. She arrived at

Sunways Farm in Housatonic no later than seven-thirty in the morning on Tuesdays and Thursdays. She learned how to shear sheep, herd pigs and feed horses. As a perk, the farm allowed her to take a horseback ride at noon when her "shift" was complete. She would often go galloping through trails and pastures until late afternoon. The resident trainer was amazed by how quickly she mastered the saddle and reins. Maddy enjoyed riding, and thought of it as an organic way of suntanning. She returned to Lenox reeking of hay and manure. After showering, she would doll herself up and wait for Jay to take her out to dinner.

Throughout the fall, Jay would bring Madison to family functions like barbecues and christenings. His inner circle was generally apprehensive about his girlfriends, but Maddy, by most accounts, was a critical success with nearly everyone she met. The Gordons appreciated her simply because Jay seemed happy.

Periodically, boxes would arrive at the house from San Francisco, and the sheer volume of Maddy's possessions astounded Jay. Since none of the boxes were ever opened, they sat idly in the garage collecting dust. Jay had Verizon install an extra phone line in the house so that Madison could have her own number. He even found her an ancient, analog answering machine so she could record a personalized outgoing message.

On a late Friday afternoon in early October, Jay stopped at home to throw on a white dress shirt. Minutes earlier, he had received a frantic phone call from one of his partners at Porter's, who told him that the floor manager had quit without notice and a server had called in sick just before one their busiest Columbus Day weekend dinner shifts. Jay was preparing himself to manage the restaurant and even wait tables to help the restaurant get through the night. He was in the master bathroom washing his face when he heard a loud smashing sound. Because he was in such a hurry, he ignored the noise until it happened again, and yet again. He noticed that Madison's car was in the driveway so he called down to make sure she was all right. There was no response. He slipped on his dress shoes and pattered hurriedly down the stairs. When he got to the living room, he noticed the deck door was completely open and the coffee table and armchair were missing.

"Mad?" he called out.

Smash! Another crash echoed from below. The end table and two paintings were also gone. Jay walked outside and found Maddy hoisting pieces of furniture and artwork off the third-story balcony.

"What the fuck?"

Maddy was hardly contrite. "I can't bear to look at this hideous shit anymore!" She was breathing heavily and sweating profusely.

Jay was furious and astonished.

"Are you fucking out of your mind? This is a furnished rental! This shit isn't even mine!"

"I don't care whose it is. It's ugly. I'm living here and I can't look at it." Albeit out of breath, she sounded reasonably calm in her explanation. Jay simply put up his hands and shook his head. "Holy fuck. You are absolutely fucking insane!"

Maddy flung a small painting at him like a Frisbee and shrieked, "Don't you ever call me insane!"

As he walked inside, he heard the painting skid across the wood paneling and land in the bushes under the deck. "Wow!" he shouted back. Nothing in their relationship had prepared him for this. He left the house wondering if this was an isolated incident or a precursor of things to come.

CHAPTER 29

The road warriors arrive at the Nashville, Tennessee, Marriott at around eleven-thirty PM. Aside from filling the gas tank twice and a quick breakfast at the Waffle House, they had not stopped since leaving the Comfort Inn in South Carolina earlier that morning.

Jay showers while Smitty rolls an enormous cone-shaped joint and sprinkles the remaining hydroponic crumbs into Axl's dinner dish. He even includes a filter at the tip, which he constructs from a loose piece of Zig Zag cardboard.

"Nice craftsmanship!" Jay notices the spliff immediately as he exits the bathroom followed by a cloud of steam. He is fully dressed, his hair slickly combed.

"You like that?" Smitty is sprawled out on

his bed and Axl is now resting at the foot.

"Hit the shower, Clyde. Let's git her dunn."

Smitty pops up, removing his shirt and tossing it toward his suitcase. "Jay-baby's sportin' the wet look tonight. You're making me horny."

Jay is not amused. "Hurry up, I'm hungry."

After Smitty's shower, Jay hears the electric hum of the hair dryer. He begins banging on the bathroom door. "Hey, Nancy! Can we work on the coif later? I wanna fucking suck down this coner and go get drunk."

Smitty shuts off the dryer and shouts back. "Fuuuuck you, doode!"

Just as they are ready to smoke, Jay pauses. "Wait. We should probably towel the door."

"Jeee-zus," Smitty replies. "Now all we need is a blow tube and a *Barely Legal* magazine under the bed and we're back at Chapman."

Jay stuffs a damp towel under the door and Smitty lights the cone, exhaling a thin stream of grayish-yellow smoke.

Fifteen hours of steady driving and sobriety only enhances the high. As the spliff burns into a roach, both travelers become bleary-eyed and giddy. Smitty drops the remnants into an ashtray and shuts off the lights. Jay slips the bottle of Demerol into his pocket as they leave the room.

At the bar downstairs, a busty woman in her twenties wearing a starchy white button-up and a black bowtie greets them.

"I'm gonna start with a Stella, please." Jay places his credit card atop a stack of cocktail napkins. The bartender nods and turns to Smitty.

"I'm gonna need a sec."

When she returns with a frothy pint, Smitty orders.

"I'll have a Red Bull Merlot with a cherry."

Jay is taking a sip of his Stella, and when he hears Smitty's deadpan request he spits out his beer and it splatters across the surface of the bar. Smitty watches Jay's reaction and cackles boisterously.

"Y'all muss be high on crack or *sumthin*!" Fortunately the bartender has a sense of humor. With a small towel, she mops up the beer spit and looks back at Smitty, who is still smirking.

"Do you have Bartles and Jaymes on tap?"

Jay is now embarrassed. "Dude, c'mon."

Smitty apologizes. "Sorry. It's been a long day. I'll just have a bottle of Bud. You don't need to bring a glass."

The bartender reaches down, pops the top of the beer and sets it in front of him. "First round's on me, boys." She winks at Jay and walks away.

"Excuse me," Jay calls back. "Can we see a couple of menus?"

The bartender looks at her watch. "At this hour, we only serve bar food and they're closin' up in about—"

Smitty chimes in. "That's fine. We'll have two bacon cheeseburgers with fries. Do you have curly fries?"

"Yeah. We shurr do. We call 'em tater fingers."

"That sounds disgusting. We'll have two orders of those. And you might as well keep these beers coming 'cause we're gonna be here for a while."

The bartender is flirtatious now. "Oh, brother. Looks like it's my lucky night."

After the late, greasy dinner, the Highway Boys switch to tequila and Corona. Cuervo 1800 is top shelf at the Marriott, but by the second shot the acidic taste no longer offends their satiated pallets. As the bartender is pouring their third shooter, Jay reaches into his pocket and softly rattles the bottle of pills. Smitty's eyes light up.

"If I wasn't married I'd make out with you right now. Gimme one of those."

They each pop a Demerol, clink glasses, hoist tequila shots and chase with gulps of Corona. By last call, they are both slumped in droopy postures, wearing intoxicated grins. Jay has been babbling on about the female mindset with Smitty serving up cynical rebuttals. Every so often, the bartender moseys into the conversation to offer "the woman's perspective." She finds them enormously entertaining, and after her shift she mixes a whiskey sour in a pint glass and takes a seat next to Jay. It is past two-thirty in the morning and the weary travelers have tied on a heavy buzz.

"My name is Becky, by the way."

Jay's palm is pressed against his cheek but he musters a slight nod. Smitty gives her a thumbs-up.

"So, y'all want to know about girls?"

"Oh yeah," Jay replies, as if a dissertation of thought went into those two little words.

"There's two types." Becky is outgoing and seems eager to share her thesis. "Girls that know what they want and never git it, and girls that git what they want and never know it."

Jay perks up. "Hmmm. That actually makes a lot of sense. Did you coin that phrase?"

"Naw, I saw it on the Lifetime channel."

So which type of girl are you?" Jay asks with more sincerity than flirtation.

"Well, that's a trick question," she replies. "Cuz every girl *thinks* they *know* what they want."

Jay bobs his head introspectively.

"The wind cries Mary," the bartender mutters with purpose.

"What's that supposed to mean?"

"It's what my daddy used to say after Maw left home when we was yung. It's a sawng is all I know."

Smitty chimes in. "It's a breakup song, isn't it?"

Almost slurring, Jay slowly recites the lyrics of the Jimi Hendrix song. *"A broom is drearily sweeping up the broken pieces of yesterdays life. Somewhere a queen is weeping, somewhere a king has no wife.* Definitely sounds like a breakup song."

"Well heck, I'm juss a barkeep at the Marriott Hotel. I ain't even got a man, so I know the wind ain't cryin' for me."

As Jay thinks about it, the sentiment resonates. *"And the wind cries Mary."*

"More like the wind cries Maddy," Smitty mutters, and winks.

CHAPTER 30

By winter, Madison had fallen into an unmitigated depression. She no longer met Jay at the restaurant for breakfast and stopped working out with the personal trainer. Once the weather turned cold, she quit her job at Sunways Farm, slept late and started drinking vodka throughout the day. Subtly, she gained weight around her hips, which made her too self-conscious to go to the spa for a professional grooming. This resulted in the disintegration of their sex life. It was as if her reclusive alter ego, the same vacant being who had stared at the carpet at the Berkeley Hotel, had regained its throttle on her mind.

Jay was unwaveringly supportive during this downturn. He would often rearrange his schedule so he could come home and make her lunch or take her outside for a walk. Routinely, he would arrive at the house before noon and find Maddy either lying down drunk or still asleep in bed. One night, after literally dragging her to his parents' house for dinner, he found a bottle of his mother's Vicodin, left over from her recent knee surgery, stuffed in Maddy's coat pocket. Jay was incensed, but in his efforts to remain positive he pretended he did not notice.

Since he was out working all day, he thought it might be healthy for Maddy to have a companion around the house. From his office at Porter's, he researched animal shelters in the surrounding area and found one across the border in New York State, forty-five minutes west of Lenox. When he came home that night to break the news, he found Maddy passed out on the couch in a T-shirt and pair of panties. VH1 was blaring over the surround sound. Jay shut it off and gently shook Maddy. When she rose, Jay could smell the liquor on her breath.

"What time is it?" She squinted and scratched her disheveled hair. "Did I miss Oprah?"

"Uh, unless Oprah's on Letterman tonight, I'd say you missed her by about seven hours." Jay glanced at his watch. It was nearly eleven. "But I have something to tell you."

He caressed her arms and cuddled her. "So I was researching animal shelters because I thought it might be nice for you to have a dog."

Maddy's pale, vacant stare softened, and her crusty lips tilted into a tiny smile. Before bed, she even suggested going out to dinner on Friday night, which would be her first public appearance in over six weeks.

At Porter's, Maddy quickly drank four glasses of Sancerre and became inappropriately frisky. While they were eating, she kept reaching under the table trying to grope Jay's package. Although it was nice to finally see Maddy more vivacious, it made him uncomfortable. Under his breath, he warned her several times to stop, which only seemed to inspire her advances. Finally he got up from the table and signaled to the server that they were finished. Maddy refused to leave. Desperately trying to avoid an ugly confrontation, Jay whisked her plate away and stormed to the kitchen to wrap it in a to-go container. When he returned, Maddy was outside smoking a cigarette she had bummed from a young bar patron. Jay grabbed her hand and steered her toward the car, tossing the lit cigarette on the street. On the ride back to Lenox, she cried hysterically, and once again, Jay consoled her.

Maddy woke Jay early the next morning. She was slightly hung over but too anxious to sleep. It was a blisteringly cold Saturday and the clouds in the sky were brittle and gray. Jay made a pot of coffee and printed out the MapQuest directions, electing not to shower until later. It was a fortuitous decision.

The animal shelter was tucked in a desolate corner on a dead-end street in New Lebanon. A barbed wire fence mapped the circumference of the front yard, and a dilapidated ranch with peeling paint and loose shingles was set back from the road. Chickens and roosters roamed free in the frozen, weed-infested grass. From the car they could hear a symphony of barking dogs. Walking up to the house, the rickety stoop creaked and an eerie feeling crept over Jay. He hesitated before knocking, but Maddy was determined.

"Welcome to the jungle," he muttered under his breath.

A woman in her late forties carrying two wily cats answered the door. She was wearing a faded nightgown, a lit cigarette dangling from her mouth.

Maddy took charge. "Hi. We called about the dog."

The woman looked them over for an uncomfortable few seconds and then beckoned them inside. There were stray kittens and rabbits segregated by cages in one room. Another room contained families of large hounds and small puppies. Maddy stopped in the doorway and zeroed in on a particularly little basset hound nestled in the corner.

"You like that one, huh?" The woman read Maddy's eyes. "That li'l basset just got here last week. He ain't nuthin' more than a baby."

Jay had been eyeing the same dog. "Do you see that little guy, Jay?" Maddy's voice was more tender than usual. The woman slipped into the room and gathered the dog in her arms. Jay and Maddy began petting him incessantly.

"Look at this guy," Jay said in a baby voice. "Aaaaww. He's such a good boy. He is such a good boy!"

The woman blew a puff of cigarette smoke toward Jay's Patagonia fleece. "Maybe you'd like to look around a bit?" She hacked a hollow cough.

"No. I think we want this one." Maddy looked at Jay and he nodded, seeming eager to leave that house.

When the transaction was complete, Maddy cradled the puppy to the car and placed him in a wicker basket in the backseat. The leather upholstery was lined with a blanket, and on the ride back to Lenox, Maddy sat next to the dog.

As Jay was driving away he looked back. "You're gonna love life outside the jungle, little fella."

"You and your Guns and fucking Roses," Maddy scoffed.

"Don't you ever take Axl's name in vain!" Jay spat back with a smile. Maddy rolled her eyes as she was massaging the dog's head.

"Axl! That's brilliant!"

Maddy actually liked the name but played coy. "Dear God!"

Jay was peaking through the rearview mirror. "Look, his ears perked when I said Axl."

When they returned home, Axl roamed around the backyard, sniffing the woodpile and gnawing on the foliage. Jay pushed him playfully and he tumbled over, bouncing back nipping at his hand.

"It's hard to find a dog that is both tough and cuddly."

Maddy snapped pictures with the digital camera from Harrods.

§   §   §

Before the first snowfall, Madison traded in her burgundy Mercedes SLK 350 Roadster convertible for a fully loaded, deep green metallic BMW X5 SUV.

"I can't drive that little car in the snow," she replied indignantly when Jay questioned her about the purchase.

"You know what BMW stands for?" He enjoyed verbally jousting with her when she was in good mood. "Barely maintains in winter!"

"Oh please. You're just jealous."

He raised his eyebrows. "Yah, OK."

"C'mere Axl," she called out. "Axl loves Mommy's new car, doesn't he?" The dog yelped and came galloping in. "See, we don't listen to Daddy 'cause he's a jerk." Axl was intently licking Maddy's hand.

§ § §

The euphoria of having a dog lasted for a few weeks, but as Thanksgiving approached, Maddy was depressed again. With her deposition in San Francisco approaching, she still had not secured any legal representation. Periodically, she would receive letters and court documents from Julian's attorneys, but they sat mostly unopened on her desk in the guest room. After asking Jay to accompany her to the deposition, she never again brought up the subject of her divorce. It had been months since they'd had sex and Jay could not remember the last time he'd had his house to himself. Maddy was becoming increasingly needy as her drinking habits intensified. Some days, she would not even get out of bed to feed Axl or let him out, so Jay made special arrangements in his schedule to stop home at least once to walk the dog and check on his bed-ridden girlfriend. While removing a trash liner from the upstairs bathroom one morning, he found an empty bottle of oxycodone with his mother's name on the prescription label. He sighed and shook his head. He was beginning to feel his unconditional support waning.

He thought perhaps a change of scenery would stir the monotony and infuse Maddy with some joie de vivre. He arranged for a weekend trip to Boston and had the concierge at XV Beacon make a special accommodation for Axl because he knew Maddy would not leave her dog behind. At first, Maddy objected to the idea. "I don't want people to see me like this," she said. She was lying on top of the covers in her everyday outfit: a vintage Trunk Ltd. T-shirt and gray Juicy Couture sweats.

Jay was in the bathroom and he emerged with two scrubby poofs wrapped around his wrists. "Getting out of here will be good for you, baby. But you know what will be really good for you?" Jay began gesticulating like Mr. Miyagi waxing on and off. "Taking a shower." It was the same voice he used when he was petting Axl.

Maddy tried hard not to smile, "You're a dick." She feebly swung her hand at him and Jay caught it and pinned her shoulders down, pretending to wash her with his scrubbies. She erupted in giggles. This was her way of agreeing to go to Boston.

When they arrived at the hotel, there was a lavish assortment of flowers waiting and even a bowl full of pretzel-shaped dog biscuits. They sat around the breakfast table and chatted amicably until Jay brought up the divorce settlement. Reflexively, Maddy's head sunk and an uncomfortably stillness swelled. After some coaxing, she confessed that Julian, according to advice from his lawyers, had cut her off financially and she had been completely out of money for nearly a month. Admitting this aloud was partially liberating, but it also released a valve of clogged emotions. Tears formed in her eyes and Jay braced for a breakdown. Through relentless sobs, she narrated how pathetic her life had become; how none of her clothes fit and how she lost motivation to do anything but make herself feel numb. She stared at the chandelier on the ceiling, wishing she had the "courage to just hang herself."

"I have nothing," she kept saying.

"You have me." Jay patted her back. "You have your family. You have Axl." He stroked her hair and kissed her on her forehead.

They skipped dinner that night, as Maddy's weeping had caused swelling in her eyelids. Eventually she crawled into bed next to Jay, who hours ago had given up consoling her or trying to persuade her to go out.

The following morning, Jay offered to take her on a shopping excursion. Maddy put on a thick layer of makeup and her oversized shades. They trudged out to Charles Street and stopped at Starbucks to pick up lattes, which Madison liked to refer to as shoppers' Gatorade. Their first stop was Nickleby's Closet, a vintage clothing store. The moment they stepped into the store, Maddy, who prided herself on her expansive hat collection, spotted an Adam Yanos Kingfisher Couture feather hat on a rack in the back corner. She examined it carefully, insisting it was one of a kind. Jay glanced at the $2,499.99 price tag and nearly choked. Maddy grinned sheepishly and batted her eyes. Jay groaned, but had no real intention of disappointing her. At the register, he gave the clerk his American Express card. Maddy put her arms around him and whispered, "I love you, sweetheart." She was cheerful again, but it was disheartening for Jay to witness how a fashion accessory could transform her disposition in ways he could not.

When they got back to the hotel, she snatched the hat out of its box and positioned it on her head while gazing glamorously into the mirror. Axl came rushing over woofing, thinking the hat was a bird. He tried climbing Maddy's leg but she brushed him off with her ankle. She stood and admired herself.

"Anyone who tells you money can't buy happiness has probably never owned one of these!"

Jay was deeply conflicted about this sentiment.

§   §   §

Over the holidays, Maddy met a few esteemed members of Jay Gordon's former entourage. The night before Thanksgiving, Boca Josh was visiting from Vermont. Maddy lay on the couch with her feet up, completely sedated by liquor and painkillers. Jay decided to play a practical joke on her. He snatched the hat from her closet and brought it downstairs. He whistled for Axl, and when the dog saw the Kingfisher feathers he barked and wagged his tail vigorously. Boca laughed hysterically as he watched Axl try and attack the innocent accessory. When Maddy figured out what was happening she shrieked and ran at Jay, screaming at him to stop. She grabbed the hat from his hand and stormed upstairs, slamming the bedroom door. Boca stood there in silence, with an awkward grin frozen on his face. Jay just shook his head and walked into the kitchen to get two more beers from the refrigerator. Maddy undoubtedly expected him to come upstairs and apologize, but for the first time, he made no attempt to comfort her. Instead, he sat in the living room and talked with Boca until the early morning. Boca Josh, who had just come out of a tumultuous relationship of his own, warned Jay to be careful.

Madison was her old charming self the next day at the Gordons' Thanksgiving table. Although she had no discernable profession or social life to speak of, she was eager to make conversation and seemed genuinely interested to hear stories from Jay's siblings and grandparents. Jay's younger sister Jennifer, who was living in San Francisco while studying for the bar, chatted with Maddy about the Bay Area, and Maddy later wrote down a list of restaurants she "had" to check out. After dinner, the family migrated to the living room to have dessert and watch football. Reclining on a black Eames lounge chair, Maddy became introverted. Watching the Dallas Cowboys brought back memories of Pastor G, and at a commercial break she excused herself and tiptoed upstairs in search of Mrs. Gordon's Vicodin.

§   §   §

By the end of December, she had dug herself deep into debt. Jay opened a $20,000 line of credit in her name, which she maxed out thirty days later. On occasion, Jay referred to her as Madison Avenue, but the joke was partially on him, as he was now funding her compulsions. The week before Christmas, Maddy made a trip to New York to buy presents. She returned with her SUV filled with a lavish assortment of gifts for both Jay and Axl. For Maddy, spending money was a form of escapism, a supplement to painkillers and an alternative to psychotherapy.

She insisted that they spend the holiday at her parents' house because her three brothers would be coming home. This made Jay uneasy since her family still believed that he was simply her landlord and friend.

Jay was awoken early Christmas morning by the sound of Maddy snapping on the television and talking to Axl in her motherly voice. With her brand new Sony DV cam, she zoomed in on Jay waking up in bed and transmitted the footage over the LCD television screen, which was hanging on the wall. Once Jay was up, she focused on Axl, who was sporting a sparkly, diamond-encrusted collar.

"Jesus Christ, Mad. He looks like a prop in rap video."

"Don't take the lord's name in vain," she said in her puppy love voice. "Especially not on his birthday."

"Merry Christmas." He leaned over and kissed Maddy on the lips and she paused the camera so their kiss was frozen on screen.

"Look. It's my big Hollywood moment." She pointed to the television and tackled Jay on the bed.

"That must make you my *E! True Hollywood Story.*"

Maddy smacked him lightheartedly as she lifted off her T-shirt.

"Is this my Christmas present?" Jay was only half teasing. She covered his mouth with her hand and reached for his boxers.

"Roll the cameras," Jay chirped in a muffled voice. "This is *my* big Hollywood moment!"

Their sexual positions and strange reverberations confused Axl, who had never witnessed such animalistic behavior from humans. Standing by the foot of the bed, he asserted himself with loud woofs.

"Is it weird that he's watching?" Maddy was short of breath.

"It's good for him," Jay replied. "He's learning some valuable moves." He smacked her on her backside.

"You're a pig," she panted.

§   §   §

Christmas went as well as Jay could have hoped for. As an annual tradition, Bill wore his red sweater vest and a Santa Claus hat, and Jane baked a honey ham. Madison was in unusually good spirits as she peddled the impression that everything in her life was wonderful. She even brought over her DV cam so she could document the happy occasion.

Jay sensed from the body language of Jerry, Jackie and Johnny that they knew he was not actually a landlord, but in the Horn household, everyone abided by the unspoken credo "less talk is more."

The brothers warmed up to Jay after they got back from "restocking the wood supply." From their bleary-eyed giggly-ness, Jay sensed that they had not *actually* restocked any wood. After dinner, Bill started a fire in the hearth and Jane serenaded her guests with *Amy Grant's Christmas Album*, a gift from her husband. As Jay was leaving the bathroom, Johnny cornered him in the hallway and offered to dump some whiskey into his mug of decaf. He was whispering and wiggling a tin flask like he was at a high school dance. An hour earlier, Jay had assumed that since Maddy and Jane were whacked out on painkillers and the brothers were all stoned, he and Mr. Horn were the only representatives of sobriety.

"Why not," he whispered back and fetched his coffee cup, which had grown cool on the kitchen counter. A few scotch and javas later, Jay was whistling along to the festive crooning of Amy Grant.

By nightfall, Maddy was passed out on the couch, exhausted from holiday revelry and codeine. Jackie had the presence of mind to lift up his sister and drape her coat over her shoulders. Jay took it from there.

"Well," he addressed the room, choosing his words carefully, "I should probably take her back to *her* house." Maddy was practically asleep on her feet. "It was nice to see everyone. Merry Christmas!"

Jane voiced her futile concerns. "Are you shure yu're not too tired to drive? We have a pull-oot soo-fa…"

"Oh, that's very kind of you," Jay replied, noticing her North Country inflection. "I'll be fine."

The brothers all shook Jay's hand and patted him on the shoulder approvingly. Bill was nodding off in his easy chair in the corner.

"Welp," he cheerfully muttered. "Careful drivin'."

"Thank you, sir. Nice to see you again." Jay made his exit and helped Maddy into the passenger seat of her BMW SUV. On the ride home she leaned across the console and kissed him on the cheek.

"Thank you for being so wonderful," she whispered sleepily.

CHAPTER 31

It was a rainy Saturday in early February and Jay sat at the breakfast bar reading the *Berkshire Eagle* and sipping coffee. Maddy awoke around 11:15 and he heard the hardwood floors upstairs creaking from her footsteps. Curious because she had not come down yet, Jay walked to the bottom of the staircase and called out, "Mad? What are you doing up there?"

"I'll be right down!" she hollered back.

When she appeared in the kitchen, she was fully decked out, from head to toe, in brand new North Face hiking gear. Jay looked up from the newspaper and burst out laughing. "What the hell is this?"

"I'm going hiking, wanna come?" Although Jay knew she would never go hiking alone, he was elated. Normally, a wet, cold outdoor activity that did not involve spending money would not appeal to Madison Horn. Jay walked up to her and kissed her on the cheek. "You look adorable."

Amidst a sea of Maddy's unopened boxes in the garage, he dug up some old galoshes and a thick, yellow rain slicker. Maddy filled a backpack with dry food rations and emergency survival supplies. She was carrying an umbrella that had a compass attached to its base.

"We're hiking Mount Greylock, Mad, not scaling the Ozarks."

"Quiet. I'm prepared for anything."

Jay was amused. "Yeah. You look like a walking Mountain Dew ad. Why don't I pull the Xterra around back and you can parachute in through the moonroof."

She whacked him on his leg with the umbrella.

"Ouww. The fuck?"

"I'll drive," she muttered.

Things had been going well the last six weeks. With help from Jay's sister Jennifer, Maddy had found a lawyer in San Francisco and initiated correspondence with Julian's attorneys regarding the settlement. Although a date for the deposition had not been set, Madison seemed on top of her responsibilities again. Jay even noticed a stack of organized legal documents on her desk in the guest room. Somehow she had also convinced Julian to reinstate her monthly allowance, claiming entitlement because they were technically still married. With her first installment, she paid Jay back a portion of the money she had borrowed from him. Jay was impressed by her acumen and equally amazed by her ability to bounce back from a long spell of depression. Although she was still somewhat nihilistic and hyperconscious of her body image, she was eager to go out to dinner again and take occasional trips to New York and Boston. With Porter's and Maison running efficiently, Jay had more flextime away from the restaurants.

Jay, Maddy and Axl piled into the X5. Maddy programmed her GPS for Mount Greylock, one of the highest points of elevation in New England. A merciless hail pelted down on the windshield of the BMW and the wipers whooshed at a furious pace. In the backseat, Axl slid from side to side, pawing and growling feebly at the noisy rain, his hot breath making little steam clouds on the windows.

Jay was in good spirits. He extended his palm and patted Maddy's leg reassuringly and she looked at him briefly and smiled.

Depending on the hiker's ambition, Greylock has both steep hiking trails and meandering paved roads, all of which lead to the lookout tower at the top. Given the conditions, they chose a more prudent approach, driving three-quarters of the way up and parking where they could see the mountain's peak. The weather did not seem to deter Axl and he sprinted around fervently, sniffing moss and scraping small holes in the frozen dirt. By the time they reached the tower, their cheeks were cold and rosy and a frosty mist clung to Maddy's hair. Jay lifted her up and hugged her vigorously. His tingly nose pressed against her warm neck and the familiar scent of TRESemmé shampoo permeated his nostrils. He inhaled deeply, as if to savor the moment and utterly appreciate the girl in his arms. A harsh wind blew prickly hail droplets sideways but Jay barely noticed. Gazing out at the tiny, picturesque sprawl of Berkshire County, he had an epiphany. Without a filter, he thought aloud.

"Why don't we start a restaurant together?"

Maddy's jaw dropped. "Oh my God, baby! Do you think we could?"

"I've had this concept for a while but I can finally see it now."

In the freezing rain, standing at the apex of Massachusetts, Jay narrated his vision.

"I want to open a surf shack pizza joint. We could be business partners." The more he spoke, the more it made sense. "You could design the interior. I'm thinking surfboard countertops and fake palm trees. I'll write the menu. We'll make pizzas with names like Surf the Goat, Pipeline Pepperoni, and our signature pie, Nikythefelon. We'll serve buddy boy hot wings, fish tacos, and Baja burritos the size of footballs. It will be a career; an investment; an asset; a labor of love." He paused as his excitement waned for a prophetic reflection. "It's fate, Mad. I mean, I named my first restaurant Maison—before I ever even knew you—and Maison means home."

Maddy was smiling, with tears in her eyes.

"And you are as much of a Maison—"

She put her index finger on his lips and leapt into his arms.

In this moment, they shared what Jay would later refer to as "the-plane-is-crashing-and-we're-about-to-die" kiss.

This day would haunt Jay Gordon for many years to come.

CHAPTER 32

Nantucket's three-letter airport code and Axl's short, phonetic name became the inspiration for Ack's Pizza Shack, the business moniker of Jay and Maddy's joint venture. Jay returned from Mount Greylock with a renewed sense of purpose. All the uncertainties he had been harboring about his relationship evaporated on that hike. His perspective changed. He believed in his heart that Maddy was only limited by her lack of direction, and that building a business together would provide her with her own renewed sense of purpose. In a matter of days, his attorney drafted the appropriate paperwork and he secured a unique loan agreement that stipulated he would provide the entire down payment for the partnership until Madison's divorce was finalized. Throughout the day, while he was working at Porter's and Maison, his thoughts were consumed by the layout and menu of Ack's.

However, almost paradoxically, Maddy turned back into a bedridden recluse. It was almost as if she resented Jay for investing in her. She began drinking from the moment she woke up, which was never before ten AM.

"I don't do single digit wake-ups," was her flippant response when Jay asked her to get up to early to come look at a possible space for their restaurant. She was not deliberately trying to sabotage Jay's plan, but subconsciously she withdrew from the responsibility.

One morning, Jay stopped home after his workout and found Maddy lying under the covers watching a movie. A Smirnoff and tonic and a bottle of pills were positioned on the night table.

Internally, Jay sighed. "Breakfast in bed?"

"Just leave," she replied.

Several issues of *Tatler* magazine were strewn across the bed, and a virtual filmography of Meg Ryan DVDs lined the floor by the dresser. Attempting to clear the bed, Jay began gathering the magazines.

"What do you think you're doing?" Maddy sipped her drink without taking her eyes off the screen.

"Fucking *French Kiss* again? You just watched this two days ago!"

French Kiss, about an American girl who travels to France to confront her fiancé but meets a charming European criminal whom she ends up falling for, had practically been on repeat for the last week.

"Please leave me alone, Jay."

"All these movies are overdue. Why don't you get out of bed?"

Slowly, Jay was losing his patience. He wanted desperately for Maddy to take part in the process of creating Ack's, but he realized if he kept nudging her in that direction, it would have an adverse effect.

Later that evening, as Jay was returning *Joe Versus the Volcano* and *Prelude to a Kiss,* he noticed a "For Commercial Lease" sign in an empty window next to the video store in downtown Lenox. Instinctively, he called Maddy from his cell phone and without revealing any details, asked her to meet him in town. She came, mostly out of curiosity, but when she saw the vacant storefront she tilted her head to the side and looked at Jay lovingly.

"It's amazing." She leaned down and put her cheek on his shoulder. It was a clear, brisk night and Jay took his scarf and wrapped it loosely around her neck, so they were attached by Hermes cashmere.

"I'm sorry I've been such a bitch lately," she whispered.

Jay squeezed her without responding.

They signed the lease the following afternoon.

§   §   §

The date for the deposition arrived by mail, via a large legal envelope with the engravings of the five-name law firm representing Julian. Jay sat beside Maddy as she opened it and read aloud the specifics. It turned out she had less than seven weeks to prepare. Jay encouraged her to call her lawyer immediately to start building a time-sensitive strategy. Maddy's face grew pale and she seemed nervous and fragile, insisting she needed a drink before doing anything else. He fixed her a Sapphire and tonic, kissed her on her forehead and left for a staff meeting at Maison.

Later that evening when he returned, Maddy had not moved from her spot on the couch nor had she called her attorney. The translucent, aqua bottle of Bombay gin was tipped over on the coffee table, and Axl lay next to her licking her ankles. When Jay lifted her up and carried her upstairs, his jarring footsteps woke her. She groaned loudly and called out, "Bathroooooooooooom!"

He brought her to the upstairs bathroom and held her hair back as she vomited into the toilet.

"Jesus, Mad. How much did you drink?"

Her slow, deliberate breaths sounded as if she had just hiked a massive incline. She was sweating and her body temperature was balmy. Again she heaved forward, almost pounding her head on the porcelain rim. The thud of bucketing liquid was especially troubling to Jay.

"Did you eat anything today? Other than painkillers?"

She took one final gasp and slumped to the floor, covering her head with her arms. Jay brought in a pillow and a blanket and propped her cheek up so it was not pressed against the cold marble tile.

Before sunrise, Madison shook Jay, who was sound asleep.

"Aspirin! I need aspirin!" Jay woke up instantly.

"There's none in the bathroom? OK, baby. OK. Look in the kitchen. There's a bottle in the cabinet with the spices."

Maddy came back to bed, swallowed four pills and placed a tall glass of water on the bedside table. She flopped down next to Jay, who had fallen back asleep.

He woke up two hours later and saw Maddy was shivering in her sleep. He covered her with an extra quilt and left the deposition letter next to the bed as a palpable reminder for when she woke up.

After cashing out at Maison he drove to Great Barrington for a manager's meeting at Porter's. Jay returned to Lenox to meet with an architect about drawing the blueprints for Ack's. Optimistic that she was feeling well enough to sit in on the meeting and perhaps provide insights on the designs, he called her at home and left several messages on her cell phone. She never responded.

By the time the Jay pulled into the driveway, the sun hovered behind the mountains like a blurry pumpkin, bleeding in the wintery horizon. All the lights in the house were off and Maddy's X5 was in its usual spot.

Jay stepped inside and dropped his keys on the coatrack table stand.

"Mad!" he called out.

Axl came bounding down the stairs. Jay noticed that Kingfisher Couture feathers were stuck to his back.

"Mad?" he called again.

He kicked off his shoes and walked into the living room.

"Maa—!" He swallowed his third call, nearly tripping over Maddy, who was passed out on the floor in a drunken lump, camouflaged by the shadows.

The living room looked like it had hosted a wrestling match between a turkey and a peacock. Strewn around the room were the remnants of Maddy's precious Adam Yanos hat, which Axl had eagerly ripped apart and chewed into a slobbery pulp. Jay flipped on the lights in the kitchen. The garbage had been toppled by the weight of five empty Heinekens and a broken bottle of Dom Perignon, which Jay had bought recently and hid in the back of the refrigerator to celebrate breaking ground at Ack's. A fly feasting on the spill flew away when Jay slapped the refrigerator's exterior.

"Madison!" he roared, his hand stinging from the impact.

"This is fucking bullshit." He whisked the garbage can back to an upright position. Banana peels and coffee grinds fell at his feet. Frustration simmered throughout his frame. As he tossed the bottles into the recycling bin, anger bubbled over like the sticky champagne residue on the kitchen tile. He stormed over to Maddy and shook her vigorously. Limp as a human slinky, she was unconscious and did not respond. Small sediments of drool clung to the corner of her mouth. Mrs. Gordon's painkillers were scattered across the rug and the prescription jar was empty in her hand. Jay panicked. Furiously, he dialed 911, remembering her occasional intimations about committing suicide. She was still unconscious when the ambulance arrived to cart her to Berkshire Medical Center in Pittsfield.

Dehydrated and malnourished, she spent the night in the hospital hooked to an I.V. pumping fluids into her veins. Jay followed the ambulance in his Audi and sat by her bedside all night until her outpatient release was granted early the next morning. The ride home was still and silent. Maddy would not even look in his direction.

When they pulled into the driveway, Jay shut off the ignition and turned to her.

"You need help, Mad."

The air had been sucked out of the car. Having not slept, Jay's ire from the night before lingered wearily and was balanced by his reluctant empathy.

"It's so fucking embarrassing you called a fucking ambulance. I just want to fucking die." Her skin was pallid and her voice shivered with expressionless animosity.

Jay remained composed and coherent. "I just spent the night sitting next to your gurney watching you wheeze in your sleep as an intravenous dripped vital nutrients into your arm. We're way passed worrying about your embarrassment. You need to get some fucking help." As the words came out of his mouth, his conviction formed. Maddy's precedent for managing depression had eroded over the last six months and Jay realized that he should have pushed for this much sooner.

Maddy stared at the gravel driveway and her eyes welled. Finally she turned and looked at him. "Fuck you, Jay." Her tone was soft and sober. "Why do you even care?" She started sobbing without uttering a sound. "No one has ever cared about what happens to me," she spat.

Jay took her hand between his palms and looked her squarely in her watery eyes. "No one has ever taken the time to get to know you, Madison."

He took off his coat and draped it around her like a blanket. After a few moments, he walked around the car and opened her door, extending his hand. She grabbed it, and he pulled her up and guided her slowly into the house. They went directly upstairs to bed. Jay was exhausted and resolved to fall asleep without further discussion, but Maddy spoke.

Tears rolled gently down her cheeks. For the first time in her life, she took a psychological leap.

Sometimes when you live without acknowledging the experiences that have shaped you, the past becomes a slow train of suppression that eventually overtakes the present. Or perhaps in this moment Maddy was too fragile and tired for pretense and too humbled by the circumstances. She began by speaking about her mother's reclusion and anxiety; moving from Leeland to Lenox and not having any friends; meeting Pastor G and the children at Faith First. Jay slid up sideways in bed. Almost metaphorically, a beam of morning sun broke through drapes, illuminating the night shadows on the windowsill.

Maddy spoke about brainwashing and attempted deprogramming; missionary work in the Caribbean; her first marriage in Maryland, and life in New York as a newlywed working to support her husband. Jay listened intently, occasionally offering compassionate sighs or wistful smiles. She spoke about the Darwinistic world of corporate lawyers, hedge fund managers and venture capitalists; trips to California; her second marriage; the night she met Jay; living in London; moving back to Lenox, and finally, her second divorce.

Although Maddy was careful to omit specific details and time periods, she provided Jay with an infusion of clarity and cognitive fodder, giving him a conduit between who she really was and the way he interpreted her. Having never spoken to anyone about her past, Maddy felt as if she had plunged from a precipice.

When her words trailed off, Jay lay back down and symbolically opened his arms. Maddy settled her head on his chest, and the aftermath of this dialogue was digested subconsciously, as they both slept soundly until late afternoon. When they awoke, a surreal level of comfort hovered in the atmosphere. They shared a rare, unspoken understanding of each other that made conversation unnecessary. They showered together and drove to Bennington, Vermont, for dinner. Jay was resolute about finding Maddy professional help and knew that her ability to prepare for the deposition and contribute to Ack's would determine her psychological progression. And once again, he became cautiously optimistic about their relationship.

§   §   §

Maddy researched the celebrity "wellness center" she had read about in *W* magazine. Located in the serene canyons of Los Angeles, Horizons Malibu is a Betty Ford-esque clinic for hippy-Hollywood types who seek resolutions to anything from bulimia and homophobia to heroin and fetishism. It is a weeklong program with a voluntary, open-air atmosphere that provides a strict diet of organic vegetables and toxin-free meats, and regimented routines of exercise and yoga. She presented Jay with the idea of going a week before the deposition so the California trips could coincide. The problem was that Maddy was broke again, and this "rehab" cost $5,500 for six days and seven nights. Encouraged by Maddy's willingness to confront her depression and substance dependencies, Jay took the initiative. In lieu of the three-month waiting list at Horizons, he called twice a day for two weeks until, by sheer happenstance, a cancellation opened a slot for Maddy the very week before she needed to be in San Francisco. Jay used the American Express card in her name to make the arrangements. He also booked a flight for himself a week later.

Maddy flew out on a Sunday afternoon. Hours before her flight, Jay cooked her a private brunch at Maison and drove her to the airport in Albany, peppering her with positivity along the way. She seemed excited and her demeanor was relaxed and upbeat, at least for the time being.

CHAPTER 33

Having slept for less than an hour, Jay and Smitty are woken suddenly by the abrasive strobe light contractions of the fire alarm. Axl is howling at the foot of Jay's bed but his barks are swallowed by the shrill, staccato alert horns. A well-worn beer buzz supplemented by tequila, hydroponics and Demerol—enhanced by fifteen hours of driving on four hours of sleep—makes it difficult for them to get out of bed. But the alarm is too deafening to ignore. Disoriented and surly, Smitty lumbers to his feet and slips on his hotel-issued bathrobe. Jay instinctively cups his ear with one hand as he fishes for Axl's leash.

Sweat is beading from their brows as they step out of the room and trudge down the hall. Smitty lifts a white cloth hood over his head like a middleweight fighter sauntering into the ring. Axl charges ahead but Jay grips his leash, restraining his progress. The earsplitting noise continues in unison throughout the hotel. When they arrive at the elevators, Jay catches his refection in the shiny gold doors and is startled to see he is wearing only boxers and slippers.

"Fuck," he mutters. About to punch the down arrow on the elevator, something occurs to him. "Can't use the elevator if there's a fire."

Smitty turns and notices Jay's lack of apparel but is too exhausted to heckle. Axl continues aggressively sniffing the carpet ten paces ahead, keeping his leash straight and taut.

Smitty and Jay yawn in synchrony.

They both turn at the sound of a door slamming, and four police officers rush toward them from the stairs. Jay clutches Axl's leash, immobilized by the confusion. An inebriated fog compromises his vision and his eyes wander from east to west.

A uniformed cop wearing a silver badge addresses them. "What the fuck is this? What's your room number, sir?"

Smitty is staring intently at the wall, almost oblivious to his surroundings. Jay blinks and realizes an agent of the law is speaking.

"Hello! Your room number?" the cop repeats sternly.

"Oh, I'm sorry." He reaches down to where his pocket would be, plucking at the tight cloth of his hybrid underwear, searching for a room key. The other three officers have scattered down the hall, beating on each door with their billy clubs as they pass. The sonic contractions of the alarm are still deafening.

"Uh, Smit?"

Smitty wipes his face vigorously with his palm.

"Do you have the key card?"

Smitty shrugs his shoulders. The cop is impatient. "Come with me," he says abruptly.

They look at each other in bewilderment. Normal brain activity is beginning to resume as they march down the hall in formation.

"And where's your goddamn clothes?" the cop barks.

Jay turns back to Smitty and mouths the words, "I don't have the fucking room key," shaking his hands in the air helplessly. Smitty takes the reins.

"Sir. I mean no disrespect, but would you mind telling me what is going on?"

The cop continues walking, shaking his head in aggravation. Besides the other three officers there is no one else in the long corridor on the sixth floor of the Nashville Marriott.

Smitty taps Jay and mouths the words, "He thinks we're gay."

Jay rolls his eyes. Axl is now trotting beside him and the leash is limp.

Behind them, the same door slams again. Three more uniformed cops and two men in plainclothes and dark blue windbreakers move rapidly down the hall. The officer in the lead is a man in his early forties with a crew cut and a clean shave. He swings around and puts up his hand. Jay, Smitty and Axl stop short.

"Reinholt, any word from dispatch?" he asks one of the other uniformed cops.

"They haven't moved, far as I know." Reinholt speaks in a deep drawl and his mustard-colored mustache hangs over his upper lip. He points to the travelers without directly acknowledging their presence. "What's this, the cast of Scooby-Doo?" They share a chuckle and continue walking side by side toward the cluster of cops at the end of the hall.

"We got a fuckin' nudist, a mute and a basset hound. Other than that, the coast is clear, far as I can tell."

In the corner of the corridor, a young officer in his early twenties calls out to the two cops approaching. "Are we gonna need a battering ram?"

"Wentworth, you dumb fuck," the older officer shouts back, "did you bring a battering ram?"

"Yessir. I believe I did," he replies, clutching his genitals. "But I prefer not to use it without a female present."

"I figure the sight of this naked man should be enough for you to draw wood strong enough to knock down this here door."

As they pass room number 614, Jay pauses to see if by any chance their door is unlocked. It is not.

"Now what the fuck is INS doing down there?" Wentworth has a nasally voice that particularly irritates Smitty. Sure enough, at the opposite end of the corridor, three men in blue windbreakers are pacing back and forth.

Five uniform cops now fill the far end of the hallways gripping their billy clubs and hovering around room number 628.

"Go 'head," barks an elderly man with a

razor-shaved head. One of the officers taps firmly on the door with his stick.

"Abra la puerta!" he hollers, tapping even louder the second time.

Smitty lifts off his hood as his sense of intrigue is piqued.

Another cop steps forward with a magnetic key card and the cluster of officers part as he swipes it into the electronic reader attached to the door. A green light appears and all five cops push through the door and stampede into the room.

CHAPTER 34

The week Maddy was at Horizon's Malibu, the house in Lenox was pleasantly quiet and refreshingly devoid of human drama. She left on a Sunday, and by Thursday had yet to call. Jay assumed telephone privileges were highly regulated so he went about his business without expecting to hear from her. The following Sunday morning, he packed a suitcase and drove to Albany to catch his flight to San Francisco. The deposition was on Tuesday, which left a day to meet with lawyers and go over documents. When he arrived at the Clift Hotel, he noticed he had missed a call from Madison. Her message was lighthearted and energetic, and without a tinge of contrition she explained a group of her "program peers" would be spending some time in Pasadena, thus delaying her arrival. Jay swallowed his anger and decided to have a drink before calling her back. At the hotel bar, he sipped three Patrons slowly, ruminating over his expectations for Maddy, now that he had invested nearly $6,000 in her wellness. When his third glass was empty, he ducked into the lobby to use his cell phone.

Throughout their relationship, Jay made it a mission to keep Maddy both honest and responsible. He often checked his own ego in the interest of setting an example. But on this evening, his tequila-induced pride piloted his emotions. He took her absence as a personal affront. Crucial divorce proceedings notwithstanding, the tone of her message demonstrated a cavalier disregard for her responsibilities as a partner. Her phone rang six times but she did not answer. Jay imagined her sitting outside at some chic beergarten eating duck satay and sipping Pinot as she screened his call. He left her a prickly message that was never returned.

Early the next morning, Jay heard the hotel door creak open and the subtle thud of suitcases hit the carpet. His face was pressed into the pillow with the half-conscious fatigue of someone who had been lying awake all night.

The room itself was noisy and the drunken clamor of passersby on the street below had agitated Jay. Maddy sat down on the bed and put her hand on his bare back.

"What the fuck, Madison?" his mouth was muffled by the pillow.

Jay did not move from his position until Maddy wrestled him around. He sat up in bed and when he saw her, he immediately noticed a difference. Her hair color was lightened and she wasn't wearing makeup. Her skin was soft and delicately bronzed by the California sun. She looked nourished and fit and her eyes sparkled with vitality.

"Hey," he said in a raspy voice, clasping her hand and kissing her cheek. His anger and pride dissipated. In spite of himself, always in spite of himself, he was happy to see her.

Jay slept soundly until eleven, but realizing the deposition was less than twenty-four hours away, he got up and showered and then attempted to wake Maddy so she could handle whatever necessary legal preparations were required. Maddy, however, was utterly defiant about not getting out of bed. At first it was amusing, and Jay wrestled with her playfully until it became evident she was not going to budge. He felt his patience waning so he left the room and went for a walk. When he returned, Maddy was still in bed watching soaps. Jay flipped off the television to confront her and Maddy told him that she had spoken to her attorneys earlier in the week and they thought it might be best if she did not attend the deposition. Jay was furious.

"Then what the fuck am I doing here?" The question was partially directed at himself. "I have two businesses to run!" He paced the room and continued to let off steam. "And *we* have a business *I'm* trying to run that you have done *nothing* for!"

Maddy, who had slipped into the bathroom to brush her teeth, spit a mouthful of chalky liquid into the sink. "Stop yelling at me! What did you want me to do? They told me they didn't want me!"

"That's because you're a degenerate," Jay muttered under his breath as she turned on the faucet to rinse her toothbrush.

"What?" she fired back.

"Jesus Christ, Madison. I wanted you to call me. I wanted you tell me I didn't need to drop everything to fly out here and support you."

Emerging from the bathroom, Maddy had a timid look about her. "Well, I'm sorry." She was rarely contrite in the midst of an argument. "I thought we could spend some time together in a place I used to live."

It was also perhaps her way of reinventing

a city she associated with neglect.

For the moment, Jay chose compassion over venom. He calmed down and hugged her loosely, patting the back of her head and pretending to strangle her from exasperation. Maddy smiled and put her head on his shoulder. However, for the rest of the day, she acted as if his prudent demeanor was spoiling her "holiday." With zero money of her own, she pleaded with him to take her shopping, and when he refused she moped around the San Francisco streets like a cranky child. Having just come from a week at one of the country's most preeminent wellness centers, Jay was not witnessing the behavioral correction he had hoped for. As they were sitting down to dinner at Gary Danko, he found his temper again. Maddy had been mutely pouting for about an hour and Jay was fed up.

"This fucking sucks," he murmured, without bothering to pull out her chair.

Maddy took note and sat down. "You're just upset because I won't have sex with you," she whispered, as their waiter approached with bottled water and a breadbasket.

"This is not about sex! This is about common decency, Mad."

"Sshhhhh!" Maddy squinted, and covered her mouth with her palm.

Jay shook his white linen napkin in the

air defiantly before placing it on his lap. The restaurant was moderately busy for a Monday and the delicate strumming of a string quartet by the fireplace in the corner provided a pleasant backdrop for a quarrel. Speaking in firm, low tones, he launched into a fiery attack on Maddy's intentions and priorities, noting that she still owed him upwards of $80,000 and wondered when or if she would ever do anything for Ack's. She sat and listened but became too indignant to remain at the table. Jay was mid-sentence when she stood up and strutted out of the restaurant without another word. He stayed and ate by himself, enjoying two bottles of Cabernet, and chocolate soufflé for dessert.

They slept in the same bed at the Clift that night but did not speak to each other. On Tuesday, Jay caught a cab and boarded an early flight back to Albany. Maddy followed a day later.

Remorsefully, on Thursday morning she got up earlier than usual and drove to the construction site for Ack's. Jay was at Porter's and all the builders and architects were hesitant to provide her owner's access since they had never seen her before. When Jay arrived later that afternoon, he chuckled to find Maddy wearing old Levis, dirty work boots and an oversize yellow hard hat. She scampered up to him and stood on tiptoe to kiss him on the cheek.

"Thank you," was all she whispered.

Jay could decipher the rest.

That evening, for the first time in over a month, Jay and Maddy made a public appearance in Berkshire County. They dined at Maison and Maddy spoke almost anecdotally about her week at Horizon's Malibu.

In her story, she repeatedly referenced a man named Desmond McDermott, whom she called Des or Desi. He was a producer and manager of seminal British bands from The Who to the Sex Pistols. Oxford educated, he had spent nearly thirty years as a music mogul in New York City before retiring in England. Most of the time he stayed at his country home in Yorkshire, but (and here Maddy used her old man Brit voice) "when feeling up for the urban rigmarole," he maintained a townhouse in the Notting Hill section of London.

By her description, he sounded like a pretty pathetic figure, bald and rotund, with an appetite for overindulgence so robust it had landed him at a pristine rehab facility in Los Angeles. Madison seemed impressed by his wealth and affluence but paradoxically compassionate about his loneliness and repellent bravado. Jay observed that when speaking about Desi, she loosened her vocal tones as if she were addressing a small child.

She also spoke of Carla Stone, a self-described Ivy League JAP whose husband was a managing director at Pacific Strategies, a private equity firm based in Santa Monica. She was a conflicted housefrau whose education and aristocratic upbringing gave her a defiant attitude toward her husband's neglect. She attributed her eating disorder and Lithium dependency to the superficiality of Beverly Hills socialites. Maddy enjoyed Carla's company, in part because she reminded her of Rachel Rothstein, but more so because she reminded her of herself.

Without saying so, Jay understood that embracing the connection of commonality was part of the cachet of such a retreat, but he wondered how mingling with affluent codependents would ultimately affect Maddy's psyche.

Over the next month, it proved to be a valid concern. Maddy developed a strange pattern of behavior. She would often get up before Jay, and as he was getting ready for work he could hear her talking quietly on her personal phone line in the guest bedroom. Although he found this odd, he never questioned her about it. He assumed she was simply talking confidentially with a sponsor or program peer from Horizon's. One evening at dinner, Maddy announced that her friend Carla, from the group, had asked if she would accompany her on an all-expenses-paid yoga retreat in Cordoba, Spain.

"Should I go?" she asked with wide-eyed innocence.

"Uh, wow. Yeah! That sounds amazing!" Jay tried to seem enthusiastic, but at the same time he was thinking about her divorce settlement, her commitment to Ack's, her debt obligations and her utter lack of career motivation. Nonetheless, his endorsement was what she needed to hear. Later that night they had sex for the first time since Christmas.

The day before her flight, they drove to Boston to spend an evening together before her ten-day trip. As usual, Jay had flowers and a note waiting in their suite at XV Beacon. They ate at Number 9 Park, one of Madison's favorite restaurants on the East Coast. They had sex again that night and Jay noticed that Maddy had gotten a professional bikini wax before she left Lenox.

CHAPTER 35

The Marriott alarm has stopped ringing. The clean shaven Officer Putnam, who
is seemingly in charge, leads the stampede
of officers. Jay, Smitty and Axl peer in but
the room is dark. The officers, however, are
quick to convey their dismay.

"Empty!"

"Gotdamm cockroaches!"

"They must have been tipped off!"

Two of the officers step back into the
hall.

"Hey, Reinholt!"

"Yessir?"

"Where's the manager on duty?"

"I believe she's outside with everybody else."

"You mean everybody else except the three douchebags standing in the hall right now."

"Yessir. Everybody except the two douchebags in the hall."

"The three douchebags in the hall!"

"Sir. There is a dog in the hall."

"Reinholt."

"Yessir."

"Are you questioning my judgment?"

"No, sir. It's just, that dog is at the behest of his owner, so I hesitate to refer to it as a douchebag."

"Where are my fucking Mexicans, Reinholt?"

"I don't know, sir."

"Why don't we ask the manager on duty?"

"Good idea, sir. Should I take the douchebags with me?"

"Yes, Reinholt. Why don't *all three* of you douchebags, *and that dog*, go find me the manager."

"Yessir."

Smitty and Jay look at each other in disbelief. Reinholt approaches and as he is about to speak, Smitty interjects.

"We heard."

"Come with me," he mutters gruffly, intent on flexing what little authority he has.

"Uh, Officer Reinholt?" Smitty rubs his eyes for effect. "Do you think it would be possible for us to have a word with that manager as well? We accidentally locked ourselves out and—"

"I have to ask," Reinholt says, a hideous smirk surfacing on his face, "are you fuckers queer?"

"No!" Jay responds swiftly.

"The elevators should be running by now," Reinholt says. He pushes the down button and leers at the road warriors with mocking disapproval.

In a feeble appeal, Smitty points to Jay's lack of clothing. "You really gonna make him walk outside like this?"

As they step into the elevator, Officer Reinholt scratches his jowls and chuckles to himself.

Outside, the early morning humidity is like a steam room. The parking lot is dimly lit and crowded with evacuees wearing pajamas, or less, standing around awaiting instructions from the police. Squad cars with the Nashville PD logos are jackknifed throughout the driveway, and the blue and red swirling lights give the effect of a parking lot discothèque. Employees of the hotel are huddled together under the carport by the front entrance. Reinholt addresses the concierge in a green Marriott uniform.

"Who is the manager on duty?"

The concierge hesitates, "June Baylor, sir."

"Is she here?" Reinholt welcomes being called sir.

"She's over there trying to keep the guests calm."

"Thank you."

Reinholt marches on. Jay and Smitty lag in the backdrop.

"Axl, stay here!" Axl has spotted another dog in the parking lot and is stretching his leash eagerly. Jay hovers behind Smitty, embarrassed to exhibit his nearly naked physique.

Smitty is growing exasperated. "What the hell is going on here?"

"Looks like an INS raid gone wrong."

"Did you see inside that room?"

"No, did you?"

"All I saw was about fifteen hotel cots lined up on the floor."

"Holy shit, are you serious? 'You think they all work *here*?"

"Here or elsewhere in Nashville would be my guess."

"Why evacuate the entire hotel to seize

fifteen illegals in one room?"

"Who are you? Anderson Cooper? Maybe they're trying to make an example of the Marriott Corporation."

"At four in the morning, dude? I don't see the CNN vans."

Five cops and the three INS agents in blue rain slickers appear in the lobby inside the hotel. Officer Putnam leads them outside and tips his cap when he sees Jay, Smitty and Axl.

About ten minutes later the announcement is made that everyone can return to their rooms. It takes the road warriors an extra forty-five minutes to get a replacement key from the manager, who is inundated by questions from the INS agents. It is daybreak by the time they are back in their suite. Smitty flips on SportsCenter and rolls another joint. Jay drops some dry food in Axl's bowl and he gobbles it immediately. They are both too exhausted to fall asleep, but a few puffs of ganja help resurrect their floundering intoxication.

"What a fucking night," Smitty mumbles out of the side of his mouth as he lights the spliff.

CHAPTER 36

At around a quarter to five in the morning, Jay received a call on the house phone next to his bed. He answered in a throaty tenor.

"Hell-o?"

"Hey, it's me!" Madison was chipper.

"Are you OK?" Jay was barely conscious.

"Yeah, I'm at breakfast in London. We had a layover at Heathrow and we're crashing on the floor of one of Carla's friends."

"You're in London?"

"What's the matter? You sound angry?"

"Mad, it's four o'clock in the morning."

"I thought you'd be happy to hear from me."

"I am. I'm half asleep though."

"So, how's Axl?"

"He's fine."

"So, what are you guys gonna do today?"

"I don't know. Work. Can I talk to you later? This is kind of rid—"

"Yeah. OK, love you too, Daddy. Mmmw-wwa."

The phone went dead.

"Mad? Madison? Madison?" He hung up, perplexed. Scratching his head sleepily, he rolled over in bed.

A week later, six postcards, all from London, arrive at the house at the same time. Two were addressed to Axl but the other four were loving, thoughtful notes for Jay. At the end of each, Madison had written: *miss you lots, loves you more.*

Jay was touched by her sentiment and wanted to do something special for her when she arrived at Logan. So he booked another night at XV Beacon and arranged for a chauffeured Mercedes to escort them from the airport to the hotel. When she landed, he was waiting with an impressive flower arrangement and a bottle of Cristal.

As Maddy ducked into the car, Jay could tell she was in a surly mood. She sat down without even leaning in for a welcome-back kiss. Jay lifted his arms as if to say, "Did you notice my romantic overtures?"

"Tone it down," was her response. "I really don't feel well."

The backseat of the S600 Mercedes was a peanut butter suede, and from an ice bucket wrapped in a thick white towel, Jay poured two glasses of champagne. "You just got back from ten days of yoga in Spain. Why don't we toast to health?"

Before the toast was finished, Maddy had guzzled her bubbly and she stuck her arm out, signaling for a refill. Jay poured it gracefully and she brashly clinked his glass before swallowing another mouthful.

"Easy, Madison. This shit is twenty-five dollars a glass."

"Well, I have jet lag."

Jay mustered up his sweet, nonthreatening voice. "OK. What's wrong?"

Madison was silent for minute or two, but then expounded.

"I don't want to go back. The Berkshires are so provincial it's nauseating."

Instead of offering a litany of his usual positive retorts, Jay simply nodded his head, which undoubtedly confused her.

"So what do you want to do?" he finally responded.

She took a deep breath and looked toward her feet. "I need to find a job."

Jay's initial reaction was mixed. While

he appreciated hearing her acknowledge a lack of direction in her life, this concurrently implied she had no intention of working at Ack's. That night in the hotel room, they slept on separate sides of the bed.

A stack of mail and several messages from her attorneys were waiting for her when she got back. On her answering machine in the guest room, Jay overheard the lawyer's agitated messages. Maddy kept skipping ahead until the automated voice told her, "end of messages." In addition to the $86,000 she owed Jay, she had borrowed another $30,000 from her father, and her lawyers had agreed to be paid through the settlement. In addition, Maddy had a $160,000 option to purchase her share of Ack's. Jay began to wonder how much of this settlement would actually be left.

The answer came via FedEx. It was midafternoon and Maddy was home surfing the gossip blogs on the Internet. The deliveryman rang the doorbell and handed her an envelope that contained a check for $209,000, thus exonerating her from any further financial restitution from Julian Bixby. She signed for the package eagerly, and to celebrate she promptly purchased a new set of deck furniture from potterybarn.com.

It took awhile for Jay to adjust to the concept that Maddy was not going to be the recipient of a small fortune. Perhaps, somewhere in the back of his mind, he had rationalized her psychotic episodes and obscene spending habits all this time because he believed the "severance package" from her ex-husband would eventually compensate for her wild transgressions. But now, in essence, she was completely his responsibility.

The rest of her boxes from San Francisco began arriving at the house. One after another they piled into the garage, but like the others, were never opened.

Maddy's next preoccupation was finding a job in finance. She started by canvassing her old contacts in New York. Jay encouraged her pursuit, but remained silently skeptical about her prospects. In his view, she was a thirty-something girl who was married and divorced twice, with no college education and less than a year's experience in the field. But she was intelligent, charming and charismatic, and knew exactly how to make the most of her attributes.

"Having confidence in your potential makes up for a lack of credentials," was her motivational catchphrase.

"I agree, Mad," Jay rebutted. "But in your business most people have a ton of confidence, potential *and* credentials."

A week later Rachel Rothstein called to invite her to a hedge fund conference in Venice, Italy. When Maddy broke the news, she stuck out her tongue at Jay sarcastically. They were driving to Berkshire East for a game of indoor tennis.

"Wow. That is incredible!" Jay was actually surprised.

"Should I go?"

"Of course! This is what you want, right?"

"It would be a really great opportunity for me to network."

"Then go."

Although he would not say so, he was beginning to resent Maddy's fondness for flight. All of these trips, which he had been paying for, did not seem to affect her demeanor, nor did they improve their relationship. He knew that discouraging her from things like yoga retreats and hedge fund conferences would seem like he was handcuffing her, but he began to wonder where he fit into her plan. Changing in the men's locker room, his thoughts spiraled and his bitterness amplified. Having played a bit of tennis in prep school, he released his combative temper on the asphalt carpet.

"You serve!" he shouted as Maddy approached the opposite baseline.

"Can't we warm up first?" she yelled back, tilting her arms and racquet in an awkward stretch.

Jay was impatient. He snatched a ball from his pocket and whacked it across the net. "Volley for serve!"

Maddy let it bounce twice and hit it meekly to his left. Jay slid two steps and returned with a hard backhand. She chased it down and managed a high-arching lob and Jay jogged to the front of the net and set his feet. He timed it perfectly. As the ball descended, he spiked it violently toward Maddy's ankles. She squealed and jumped out of the way. Jay was already walking back to the baseline.

"I'll serve!" he yelled without turning back.

Maddy was a proficient tennis player, but could not compete with Jay's wrath. On some level she was attracted to his machismo bravado, but overall, relating to Jay as "the aggressor" as opposed to the "unconditional nurturer," was a difficult juxtaposition. After the first set, she stopped competing. Jay beat her on virtually every point until the match was over, 6-0, 6-0. On the ride home, things turned downright contentious when Maddy announced that she would not be buying her share of Ack's.

Jay gripped the steering wheel with his

left hand, extending his right thumb up sarcastically. "What are you going to use the money for? Shoes? New fucking lawn ornaments? And now what am I supposed to do? Take out another loan? And when do I get the money *you* owe *me*? When are you ever going—"

"Fuck you!" she sobbed. Jay "the aggressor" had finally run his course. "I'll give you the money. Just stop!"

The next morning when Jay got up, a check for $86,000 sat waiting for him under the fruit basket on the breakfast bar. He picked it up and read the memo: ***"Thanks for everything!"***

Maddy was gone.

CHAPTER 37

Jay walked to the kitchen window and noticed Maddy's car was not in the driveway. He glanced at the clock on the microwave: 8:37 AM. It was Saturday, and Jay had a sneaking suspicion as to where she had gone. He waited until nine before calling Rachel in New York. Rachel answered after one ring.

"Mad-is-on! Did you sleep in?"

This was all the information Jay needed.

"Uh. Hey Rach. It's actually Jay."

"Oh! I was reading the caller ID."

"That's what I figured. So I guess she's not there yet?"

"No, I actually just called her on her cell phone but it went straight to voice mail. Do you need me to tell her something when she gets here?"

Jay quickly thought of something.

"It's not a big deal, but can you just remind her that we have a liquor license hearing for our restaurant on Monday afternoon?"

Rachel had always been fond of Jay and she especially appreciated his patience with Maddy. "Yeah, I'll tell her. So, how are you doing?"

Jay paused. Those four words echoed in his head but he could not decode Rachel's intonation. Was she simply asking *him* or speaking in the plural. Could this be an indication Maddy had told her about their many tribulations? Was this Rachel's subtle way of asking whether or not their relationship was deteriorating?

"Good." His voice was full of hesitation.

To let Maddy know he was both calm and omnipotent about her whereabouts, he sent her a text message reminding her of the hearing. But Jay spent the rest of morning thinking about the broader context of Rachel's seemingly innocuous question. At the breakfast bar, he flipped through the *Berkshire Eagle* and sipped his coffee, trying to imagine his life without Maddy. It was somewhat painful, yet also liberating, and he smiled to himself as he wondered whether codependency was contagious. They had been together well over a year now and things had been difficult at times, no doubt, but was he doing well? Were *they* doing well—enough? Throughout the day, he wrestled with this simple, unsettling question.

Maddy returned on Sunday evening to pack for Venice. Jay had taken the night off and was napping on the couch next to Axl. As Maddy's car pulled into the driveway, Axl heard the tires on the gravel and he galloped toward the front door. Groggily, Jay met her in the hallway and kissed her on the cheek. They exchanged some pleasantries and then she quickly slipped upstairs to take a shower.

On Monday, the hearing was delayed two hours, so Maddy loaded her bags in the X5 and planned to leave from the courthouse. After the license was approved, she kissed Jay goodbye in the parking lot and drove away. Jay was out of sorts. He went home and played a mindless game of Frisbee fetch with Axl in the backyard.

About an hour later, Maddy appeared on the deck. Jay's eyes lit up.

"Hey!" He was not expecting her.

"Come here," she said suggestively.

Jay scampered up the steps.

"Let's go upstairs."

This could only mean one thing.

Twenty minutes later, they lay on top

of the covers breathing heavily. Maddy was sweaty and flushed. She climbed over Jay and glanced out the window. It was late afternoon. "Maybe I should stay and just leave in the morning."

Jay was still slightly out of breath. "Stay. I'll get up early and cook you breakfast."

The raw emotions of sex and vulnerability lingered in the air. "That's very sweet of you." Maddy got out of and bed slipped on her clothes. "But I gotta go." Jay nodded. He threw on some sweatpants and a T-shirt and walked her to the car. Maddy had a lump in her throat.

"Take care of Axl." She opened the driver side door and stood next to the steering wheel.

"You're only going for a week, Mad. Axl and I will be fine."

Jay stood and waved as she pulled out of the driveway. After dropping some food into Axl's plastic Guns N' Roses food trough, he trudged upstairs to watch television in bed.

He was in a comfortable half-doze when the phone in the guest room startled him. He listened to Maddy's outgoing message until the beep sounded, then hit the mute button on the TV remote.

"Hello, my little monkey. I am so looking forward to our trip. I have been werking quite late and can't wait to see you. Okee. Bye-bye. Kiss, kiss."

The man spoke with a deep Belgian inflection and his words pierced through Jay's skin like a snakebite. He gulped heavily and his heart sunk into his abdomen. He played the message over and over again, scanning through his mental lexicon of Maddy's friends and acquaintances, but found no clarity of thought. His heart was pounding as he paced the interior of the house without purpose. Everything was a blur. Unnerved, he called Maddy on her cell phone and left her a message urging her to check her machine. Maddy called back within minutes.

"I don't know what that was!" she responded defensively. "It sounded like my friend Thomas prank calling me."

"It's some coincidence that 'Thomas' knew you were going on a trip."

"I don'——Whu——Tssst——Currrrr."

"Mad? I'm losing you. Can you hear me? Can you hear me?"

All he heard was a dial tone followed by a series of shrill beeps. Jay hung up. His mind was still racing and his thoughts were primal and possessive. In that moment, imagining his life without Madison was no longer liberating and he desperately wanted to give her the benefit of the doubt. The phone rang once and he picked up quickly.

"Hello?"

"I am going to a hedge fund conference with Rachel. That is all. If you don't want me to go, I'll turn around right now and come home."

Jay sighed. "No. Go. I believe you. I trust you."

"Thank you, baby. I'll call you later, I promise. Love you."

Jay whispered the word, "Bye," as he hung up again. He was weak and his voice had lost its volume. He whistled for his Axl, who came trotting into the bedroom eagerly. Like a warm ball, he nestled atop the covers by Jay's feet.

Maddy called from the plane the following morning. She told him that Rachel had inadvertently booked the wrong flight and that they would be flying separately, one hour apart. She promised she would call when she landed in Italy. Jay was a mess. He had barely slept and kept hearing that Belgian voice echoing in his head. Before he left the house, he dialed Rachel's number in New York. No one answered.

Later that evening, on his way back from work, he picked up the mail at the end of the driveway. Inside the mailbox was a master phone bill from Verizon, listing all outgoing and incoming calls from each of the phone lines at the house. On Maddy's line, he found a propensity of calls to and from a particular foreign number. Jay scanned through the records, trying to determine a pattern. Finally, he found the call Maddy made from London. It was received at 4:46 AM Eastern Standard Time from that same number. He remembered how peculiarly that conversation had ended. A chilly, sad anger returned. He dialed the number on the phone bill. A man picked up.

"Heelu?"

Jay froze. It was the same voice.

"Heelu-oo?"

He hung up and called Rachel, using the code to block his number from appearing on her caller ID.

She answered after three rings. "Good evening?"

"Rachel. It's Jay Gordon."

"Oh God." Rachel was not supposed to have answered the phone.

"What's going on? I thought you were—" He stopped, wondering if a hedge fund conference even existed.

Silence.

Jay grew agitated. "Well, as I'm sure you can imagine, I am wondering where my girlfriend is?"

"I don't know, Jay. Please don't ask me."

"I'm fucking asking, Rachel. Where the fuck is she?"

There was a long, uncomfortable pause.

Rachel needed to come clean for her own conscience. "She's going to see someone named Fritz Vandeveld. They had an affair when she was married to Julian. I met him once when I was visiting her in London. He's some sort of ambassador from The Netherlands, or maybe Belgium. I can't remember exactly. I know he has a family of his own. OK? Please don't ask me anymore questions."

"She had an affair?"

"She never told you?"

"I gotta go." He was shaking.

"She loves you, you know."

He could not respond. He put the phone down and clenched his fists. An unearthly rage heated the flow of blood through his body and he felt the prickly stabs of deception. Without thinking, he dialed the foreign number again.

"Heelu?"

Jay took a deep breath. "Let me make this real clear for you. The girl you are waiting for is my girlfriend. We live together. We have a dog named Axl. Now, as soon as she gets there, I want *you* to call me and tell me—in front of her—that you will be a gentleman and leave her the fuck alone. She knows the number. Do you hear me?"

"Uh. Heelu? Who is this?"

"Listen, you slick limey cocksucker. You are going to call me tonight, because if you do not, I will phone your wife at your home in Holland and if you don't think I have that number, just—"

This got Fritz's attention. "Okee. Okee. I will call. As soon as she gets here."

Jay slammed the phone down and began pacing the house, occasionally punching soft objects. Forty minutes later, the phone rang.

"Speak!"

"Uh. Is this the residence of a Mr. Gordon?"

It was a familiar voice, but not the call he was expecting. "Who is this?"

"This is Walter Smith the third. Who is this?"

"Smitty?"

"Jay Gee?"

"Jesus Christ, Smit. It's been so long I didn't even recognize your fucking voice. How the hell are you?"

"Good, man. I'm living in San Diego. And I got big news, bro. Big fucking news!"

"You wouldn't believe the shit I'm going through right now."

"Did you hear me?"

"Sorry, I'm a little distracted. I actually can't really talk right now. Is there a number where I can reach you?"

Smitty was offended. "Yeah. I'll give you my cell. It's six-one-nine—"

The call waiting beeped twice. Jay jotted the rest of the number down. "I gotta take this. I'll talk to you soon." He clicked over, not waiting for Smitty's response.

"Hello?"

"This is Fritz Vandeveld. I am here with Madison."

"Put her on the phone."

Jay heard a muffling on the receiver. "He wants to spek with you." The phone was handed to Maddy.

"Jay?" Her voice was timid.

"It wasn't Thomas on the answering machine, was it?"

"Jay. It's not what you think. We're just old friends."

"Alright. Put him back on."

Fritz returned quickly. "Yes, Mr. Jay."

"Now let me hear you say it."

"Sir. Wear juss old friends. I will send her back to you without remonstration."

"Just remember, every time you look at her, I have your wife's number. We don't want things to get any uglier than they already are."

"Generally speking, blackmail is never an effective tool for neego-shee-a-shun. But, in certain circumstances, Mr. Gordon, we as men must make exceptions. Now is there anything else?"

"Keep your phone on." With that, Jay slammed the cordless onto its receiver.

After a few hours of sleepless anxiety, he got out of bed and poured himself a Patron with two ice cubes. It was three-thirty AM. Distressed and vindictive, he examined the most recent transaction history on Maddy's AmEx card. Her purchasing patterns charted her symptoms of mania and Jay began to connect the dots. Bikini waxes represented the anticipation of intimacy. A $300 charge at a Manhattan spa showed up a day before her flight to Italy. Shopping sprees were temporary panaceas for guilt or depression. A $15,000 debit from Barney's New York was charged just hours after she learned Jay had heard the message from Fritz. He also noticed a $200 transaction, converted from lire, at the duty-free Canali men's shop at Marco Polo airport in Venice.

He looked back at prior online statements and found a number of purchases from London, all made when she claimed to have been at a yoga retreat in Cordoba.

"Fuuuuuck!" he bellowed, and pounded

his fist on the desk. Axl woofed and trotted in, sensing something was wrong. Impulsively, he called American Express and promptly cancelled Maddy's card, transferring the outstanding balance to his small business account. Oddly enough, he somehow felt conflicted about cutting her off while she was abroad. But the very thought of subsidizing her escapades was maddening. His scruff was itchy on his neck and his eyes drooped with weariness.

Operating on sheer scornful adrenaline, he trudged downstairs to the basement and began opening her boxes with a paring knife. What he found was both jarring and sobering. Each box was filled with expensive trinkets, china, silverware, handbags, shoes, jackets, belts, hats—all of which she had re-accumulated since moving back to the Berkshires. Her memory was precise. Virtually every item in her inventory was from high-end boutique chains, and instead of unpacking the boxes as they arrived, she repurchased the exact same contents. He walked around the house, taking note of Maddy's furnishings and wardrobe accessories. He went back to the basement and found an identical counterpart to virtually every item. Hundreds of duplicate CDs and DVDs; Jimmy Choo shoes never worn; mink coats with the tags still attached; Marc

Jacobs bags with the same colors and patterns; sets of Korin steak knives; wine racks, and Williams-Sonoma kitchen sets.

Daylight had broken and Jay lay face-up on the cement floor, shielding his head with one of Maddy's vintage velvet pillows. The shock and enmity had worn off and his stomach was now heavy with sadness. He dozed off for a few hours and woke with an aching back but a mind full of purpose. He heaved himself to his feet, threw on some slacks and a polo knit and scampered out to his S4, grabbing his *Appetite for Destruction* CD as he left. He drove directly to Bill Horn's office at the Liberty Mutual building in Pittsfield, blaring "You're Fucking Crazy." Mr. Horn was with a client when he arrived but ended the meeting early when he saw Jay waiting in the lobby.

"Come in, Jay. Is everything OK?" Jay sat across from his desk as he latched the door. "You look like you've had some morning."

It was not quite nine AM. Jay sighed and reflexively combed his hair with his hand.

"Coffee?"

Jay shook his head, exhaled, and without hesitating, unraveled his long, chilling narrative about the sordid life of Madison Stewart Bixby nee Horn. Throughout his monologue, Bill's expression remained empty, indicating he was neither aware of nor astonished by these revelations. Jay admitted that they had been living together for over a year and apologized for his complicity. Under normal circumstances, it may have been difficult for a boyfriend to reveal such details about a daughter to her father, but Jay needed to clear his own conscious.

Jay leaned back in his seat and exhaled deeply. His throat quivered from pent up emotion. Bill sensed Jay's vulnerability and handed him a clean handkerchief with his initials stenciled in the corner.

"Thanks." Jay took the cloth but held his composure. In that same moment, his cell phone began vibrating from inside his pocket. He pulled it out and glanced at the caller ID: private call.

He silenced the vibrations and slid the phone back into his pocket. Thirty seconds later it rang again, and then again. Bill was awkwardly explaining that the information Jay had just conveyed would unduly upset Mrs. Horn and it would be best if she were not privy to the full story. Jay agreed, provided that Bill was forthcoming about them living together. When Jay looked at his phone, the screen read: one new voice mail.

"Excuse me." He stood up to listen to the message. Fifteen seconds of heavy breathing and sniffling, then an indecipherable female voice began stuttering and sobbing, struggling to conjure a coherent sentiment. The voice barely sounded human, but the gasps between words were unmistakably Madison.

"Of...a-aa-ll...pe-pep-peeple, yu-yu-yu-you a-a—are the last p-p-p-person I wanted t-tt-to do th-thi-this to... I am s-s-s-sooo s-s-s-orry, Jay."

Jay heard the anguish and remorse in her tone and it sounded as if she were drowning. He saved the message and limply shook Bill's hand as a somber parting salutation. Bill promised he would stop by the house and pick up some of Maddy's storage boxes later that afternoon.

Jay started the S4 but couldn't muster the strength to buckle his seat belt. The harsh electric symphony of "Sweet Child of Mine" flooded the airwaves and the familiar lyrics seared his fragile psyche. With his index finger, he pumped down the volume control button on the steering wheel until the song faded. Unable to drive, he pressed the side of his head on the glass window, soaking in the deafening stillness.

Jay nodded off for a few minutes and awoke with a stiff neck and an agonizing return to reality. He reached into the cup holder and pulled out his cell phone. Maison was on speed dial and he cleared his throat before calling the restaurant to inform them he would not be in. Then he scrolled through his contacts until he came upon Dr. Warren Miller, a world-renowned psychologist and close friend of the Gordon family. He decided against calling ahead and drove directly to his office at Austen Riggs.

Dr. Miller had known Jay since he was a teenager. From the moment Jay stepped into his office, he sensed his distress.

"Sit down," he said. "Don't explain anything." He poured Jay a glass of water from the cooler and set it on the coffee table. "Turn your mind off and let yourself just be. I'll be back in five minutes."

Jay sat still on the dark leather sofa and felt his weary eyes fill up. He could not remember the last time he had cried, but in one fell swoop the long dry streak was broken. Tears streamed silently down his cheeks. He reached into his pocket and found Bill Horn's handkerchief, and he dabbed his face before blowing his nose. He was overrun by so many confusing memories of Madison and nearly every thought was neutralized by his own naïveté. Now Rachel's four words seemed even more poignant than before.

When Dr. Miller returned, he told Jay he had cancelled his afternoon appointments.

Jay sipped the water and wiped his forehead with his sleeve. It took over two hours for him to explain everything. When he was finished, he played Maddy's most recent voice mail aloud.

Dr. Miller was certain Maddy suffered from manic-depression and possibly a bipolar disorder and that she needed immediate medication and therapy. He wrote seven digits on the back of his business card, encouraged Jay to fly her home, take her to her parents' house and give her the number of a female colleague who had experience with similar cases. He also stressed that since it would be Maddy's natural inclination to reject Jay's support out of her own guilt, he must disassociate himself from her until she had time to recover and adjust to the medication.

That afternoon when he got home, he collapsed on top of his bed and slept in his clothes until he was awakened by a phone call shortly after midnight.

Disoriented, Jay smacked the snooze button on his alarm clock but the ringing did not stop. He sat up in bed blinking his eyes. Sweat beaded off his forehead. His khaki pants and pique knit shirt were damp and wrinkled. Everything was dark. He looked at the alarm clock: 12:06 AM. The ringing had stopped. He sauntered downstairs and poured himself a heaping bowl of Honey Nut Cheerios. The house was hot and dry, and as he passed the laundry room he lifted off his shirt and tossed it toward the washing machine. The ringing started again, and this time Jay had more of his wits about him. He lifted up the cordless phone from the wall jack in the kitchen.

"Good evening."

A brief pause was followed by an automated voice.

"*You have a collect call from—*"

"Madison."

"*To accept charges, say yes or press one.*"

"Yes," Jay said begrudgingly.

"Hello? Jay?"

"What is it, Mad?"

"Are you fucking happy now. You've humiliated me. How *dare* you cancel my credit card! I have nothing now. How do expect me to get home?"

Jay remained calm. "Uh, Mad? It's my credit card, I pay the bill, and it's counterproductive for me to bankroll your affair."

"There is *nothing* going on between us! We're old friends. That is all!

"Where is he?"

Maddy took a deep breath. "He's gone."

"Stop lying to me."

"He's fucking gone, Jay! You scared him

when you threatened to call his wife."

"Come home, Mad." She hesitated and Jay could feel her anger shifting to sadness. "Axl misses you," he coaxed.

She mustered all the sanctity she had left. "This is so fucked up." Her voice trembled and she choked on the words.

Jay was silent. He could hear Maddy breathing steadily on the other end. Finally, he spoke.

"What do you want, Mad?"

She was weeping. "I don't know," she whimpered.

Jay had shifted to the couch and his cereal was getting soggy. "OK, well, I'm gonna go."

"No. Wait." She sniffled again but did not speak.

"Bye, Mad." Jay hung up the phone. Even a wounded ego must maintain its pride.

He dumped his cereal into the garbage and drove to Maison to eat and confer with Hugh.

§   §   §

Two days later, Maddy called from a parking garage in Manhattan. She was stranded and needed to pay before they would let her leave. She had stayed at Rachel's the night before but was too embarrassed to ask to borrow money for the parking fees. The garage would only take cash or a physical credit card, and since Maddy had neither she was unable to retrieve her SUV.

"Figure it out," was Jay's hardened response. His bitterness was beginning to congeal.

Meanwhile, Bill Horn had come by with Jane's Ford Explorer to pick up Maddy's boxes. Jay left Maddy's closet intact, but took the liberty of packing most of her stray belongings and home accessories. Bill made three trips loading and unloading her things back into the family garage.

Maddy returned from her trip to an altered reality. Since she was a little girl, she had consciously and skillfully managed to keep her family and her life choices disconnected. Now that her parents were privy to her transgressions, she felt exposed and humiliated.

Jay was outside walking Axl when he heard the engine of her BMW racing up the road. She careened into the driveway, spewing loose rocks across the freshly mowed lawn. She leapt out of the car, screaming at Jay and bawling, insisting that he had ruined her life.

"I wish I never met you!" she howled.

Jay just shook his head passively, pretending her words were not penetrating. Axl began barking from the commotion. With the wrath of a tornado, she raced into the house, gathering her makeup and toiletries, slamming each door as she passed. From outside, Jay heard the echoes of Maddy's tirade. To occupy himself, he walked over and began picking up some of the rocks in the grass.

They did not speak for a full week. On his way home from Maison one evening, Jay stopped at the florist and ordered one of his impressive flower arrangements. On the bouquet, he attached the number of the psychiatrist recommended by Dr. Miller and drove to the Horn house. Maddy's BMW was in the driveway so Jay marched directly to her lair in the garage. He knocked on the windowpane and waited awhile but heard nothing. Finally he opened the door and walked in.

"Mad? Maddy?" He tiptoed up the rickety, wooden stairs and found Madison sitting on her bed by the window. She was frail and ghostly. Her hair was knotted and uncombed. She was staring at a bulging black garbage bag by her bare feet.

Her eyes shifted when she saw Jay emerge with the flowers, and a small smile appeared on her dry, chapped lips.

Jay sat down next to her and put his hand gently on her neck. She leaned in to smell the bouquet.

"What's in the bag?" he asked softly.

Maddy's eyes watered. She reached down and opened it, slowly pulling out an old pair of sullied jeans, two muddy Reebok tennis shoes and a peach-colored blouse that was mangled, and spotted with dirt and blood.

"I was so young," she whispered.

He picked up her hand and clasped it, setting the flowers on the floor next to the bed. He stood up and pulled the business card from the bouquet and handed it to her.

"Call that number and use me as a reference," he said. "She is expecting you." Bending down, he kissed her on her cheek. "Promise me you'll call?"

Maddy nodded without looking up. Jay ambled quietly down the stairs, shutting the door behind him.

CHAPTER 38

"Huss-keeping!"

Smitty groans loudly and rolls over. The clock next to his bed reads 3:36pm.

"Huss-*keeping*!"

"Nooooo. Go away!" he yells into his mattress.

There are several soft taps at the door. "Huss-keeping!"

He sits up in bed and yells out, "Come back later, please!"

Jay is sound asleep.

Smitty takes his dirty sock from the foot of his bed and hurls it at Jay's face. It lands on his chin but he does not stir. After a few minutes, he gets out of bed and steps over Axl, who is passed out on his blanket. He settles at the breakfast nook, and from his suitcase pulls out a pack of honey-dipped cigar papers. The sandwich bag of marijuana is still on the table from the night before and Smitty pours out a healthy portion and begins breaking it up with his fingers.

"We've made quite a dent in this bag, haven't we, Axl." Axl looks up and woofs.

"Wake the fuck up, Gordon!"

Jay opens his eyes slowly. "Fuuuuuuck you, doood!" He tosses the dirty sock away from his nose and Smitty chuckles boyishly.

Eventually they decide to stay in Nashville for another night, succumbing to road-trip exhaustion. A magnificent late afternoon sun blazes down and Jay slides open the patio door.

"Twilight golf, Gordo?"

"Done!"

Inside the Range Rover, Jay opens the sunroof as they cruise to the King's Creek Golf Club. Just off the exit in a field of tall grass they spot a band of haggard young men sprinting in a pack in the direction of the hotel.

"Holy shit! Look at that!" Jay points out the window.

"What the fuck?"

"That's them! "

"You think?"

"It's gotta be." Jay slows down.

"Call Reinholt."

In unison they both exclaim, "Fuck Reinholt!"

"And fuck these hick-ass cops. I'm pullin' for the beaners."

Jay honks the horn in a staccato crescendo.

"Rapido, rapido!" Smitty hollers out the window.

"Don't be a prick."

"Just drive the car."

He pulls away, and at the intersection signals when he sees the sign to the country club.

"How's your game these days, Smit?"

"I got a solid drive but my short game is suspect. Have you been playing?"

"Last time I played, I shot a sixty-eight."

"Fuck you, you shot a sixty-eight. What, in nine holes?"

"It may have been twelve"

"That's brutal."

"It's not gonna be pretty. Did you bring the stroke sweetener?"

"Now that's a rhetorical question."

After turkey sandwiches and two Heinekens each, they roll up to the first hole in a golf cart. Smitty takes numerous practice swings as Jay powders his hands and slides on grip gloves.

In between the fourth and fifth holes, Smitty pulls out a tightly rolled blunt and lights it. Musky smoke bellows from his mouth like a steam engine.

"Mmmm. This is a tasty treat." Referring to the honey cigar paper, his speech is somewhat restrained by his inhalation.

When Jay tastes the weed cigar, he has a similar reaction. "Where'd you find these papers?"

"At a rest stop somewhere in Georgia. Which reminds me, how far do you think we need to drive tomorrow to get back on pace?"

"I don't know, Oklahoma City I suppose. But as I've said before, I'm in no hurry."

"I'm with you, bro. After these last few days, I'm fine doin' nothing but this." Smitty exhales another monstrous cloud and passes to his left.

CHAPTER 39

Madison, who had changed her name from Bixby back to Horn, underwent what she called a "psychological makeover." She replaced vodka with wheatgrass, and pain-killers with vitamin supplements. Religiously, on Tuesday afternoons, she saw Dr. Tara McGrath, the therapist recommended by Warren Miller. She was prescribed Zoloft and then Prozac, but stopped taking the medication after complaining about the side effects. Aside from the money she owed Rachel, Maddy was debt-free but essentially broke, and without the prospect of income or credit worthiness. Since Bill paid for her gym membership and medical bills and she ate all of her meals at her parents' house, she maintained little human contact in the outside world. After six weeks, as discussed with Dr. McGrath, she called Jay and nervously asked him to dinner.

Jay was ecstatic yet apprehensive. They agreed to meet at Maison at seven-thirty, and as he patted his cheeks with aftershave he felt the tingle of butterflies, as if it were their first date.

The initial greeting was predictably awkward, but once they were seated, their conversation was cordial. Maddy's range of topics was somewhat limited, but she commented on the new artwork on the walls at Maison. Since Maddy was refraining from alcohol, they both drank diet sodas and joked about "how lame they had become." Before the entrees were served, Jay went out on a limb and offered her the option of buying a ten percent stake in Ack's—if she wanted to—and even told her he would put her on the payroll if she needed something to do during the day. Maddy was actually receptive to the idea. She even suggested selling her X5 and using the proceeds to buy into the business. Jay had just leased a Mini Cooper with the Ack's logo stenciled on each door and he told Maddy she could use the company car to get to and from work.

Once again, Jay shelved his apprehensions. With Madison seemingly dedicated to her physical and emotional rehabilitation, he was convinced she was readjusting to the simplicity of a small-town existence devoid of ludicrous spending habits, alcohol and pill dependencies, international escapades and glamour mag ideals. A week later, he handed her keys to the Mini Cooper, and that night she slept in his bed for the first time in over two months.

Things were copacetic for a while. Maddy worked normal seven-hour shifts at Ack's and spent a night every so often at Jay's, but she would not sleep with him. Maddy told Jay that through therapy she had learned that for her, sex was something that needed to be "bad" or "wrong" in order for it to be enjoyable. This opened another window to their past, but also pointed to the psychological progress she had made with Dr. McGrath.

To the outside world, they classified themselves as good friends with a history, yet in Jay's mind they were working toward something greater. The Gordon family sternly cautioned him about getting too involved with Maddy before she had demonstrated consistent stability, but he was guided by his own optimism. Consequently, Jay ignored the first red flag.

Midway through the third month, Maddy stopped seeing Dr. McGrath, claiming she could not afford the sessions on her salary. When Jay offered to pay, she declined. Then, she began casually drinking wine with dinner. Occasionally, she would make coquettish comments about returning to the hedge fund world because she hated the thought of being "a local pizza girl." She had removed the license plates from her X5 and stopped paying the insurance, but had yet to sell the car or purchase her stake in the business.

Around the same time, her friend Desi from Horizon's offered her a free place to live in Notting Hill while she looked for professional work in London's financial district. Beneath the surface, Jay was dismayed, but he encouraged her to go if that was what she wanted. Before she left, she sold her BMW to cover her living and travel expenses. Jay reactivated her AmEx card, partially for emergencies, partially to track her movements.

In mid-April, Maddy booked herself a one-way ticket to London. Jay drove her to the airport in New York and reserved a room at the Carlyle Hotel. As always, a thoughtful note and a spectacular flower arrangement waited. Outside the British Airways terminal at JFK, Maddy wept.

"I'm so lucky to have you."

Jay unbuckled his seat belt and leaned across the console. He brushed her tears away with his finger and kissed her head. The smell of TRESemmé in her hair always conjured fond nostalgia.

"You better go." He motioned toward the curbside baggage stand.

Maddy turned and kissed him passionately before exiting the car.

§   §   §

That summer, Jay wrote her a letter every other day. By late June, Maddy had yet to find work or even write back. They talked only once a week, and from those infrequent conversations he could sense she was falling back into a depression. She complained about money and the difficulties of finding a viable source of income, but had yet to use her credit card. Jay reminded her that she still had an option to invest in Ack's if things did not work out, but she remained mum on that subject. On July 4th, he called her phone to wish her a happy Independence Day and reminisce about watching fireworks from a picnic blanket on Stockbridge Bowl. Maddy was poolside at Desi's château in the south of France.

"I've been so stressed out, I needed a vacation," she explained.

Jay was naturally suspicious but assumed an affair with Desi was unlikely owing to her description of the man.

In early August, Maddy called with news of landing a position as a bookkeeper at a high-end fashion boutique in Notting Hill. With Maddy's compulsions, this venture seemed so unlikely it was ironic but Jay sent flowers and showered her with encouragements nonetheless. The job lasted three days before Maddy quit, claiming she was not cut out for accounting. By the end of August, Desmond asked her to start paying rent and Maddy balked and decided to pull the plug.

Jay was sorting through a stack of mail from his office at Porter's when he came upon a letter from Madison. It had been sitting amidst credit card solicitations and supermarket circulars for nearly a week, and since he had received but two letters from her all summer, he often let his mail accumulate. The note was handwritten and her tone was forlorn. Jay had been seeing Dr. Miller on a biweekly basis, debunking his own attachments to the relationship, yet somehow a part of him still believed Maddy was finally ready to focus on her life in Lenox.

He met her at the Carlyle Hotel in New York. As ever, he had flowers and a welcome-back card waiting on the coffee table. Inside the card, he had stuffed ten hundred-dollar bills to help her get back on her feet. He was at the mini bar when he heard a feeble knock at the door. Through the peephole he saw Maddy hunched over from the weight of her bags. He swung open the door and extended his arms dramatically. She was pale and skeletal-like and she timbered wearily into his embrace. Jay sensed that the undertow of failure and incompetence had been pulling her back into depression.

In the Berkshires, they gradually resumed a quieted version of their former life. Maddy went to work at Ack's full time, and within a month had moved back in with Jay, but he could see her vitality seeping away.

It became a passive coexistence with no evidence of progression. In a conversation with Hugh late one night, Jay described himself as "just treading water aimlessly."

Hugh extended his pint glass of Guinness. "Here's to Old Man River."

Jay snickered soundlessly through his

nose, as if self-deprecating humor was his only recourse.

In late September, it felt like déjà vu when Maddy announced that her friend Lord Albert, whom she'd met at Desi's in the French Riviera, had invited her to his estate in northern England for a game-shooting expedition.

"Should I go?" she asked in the ever-familiar tone.

The all-expenses-paid trip was allegedly financed by the British lord himself, and Maddy claimed it would be nice to experience "luxury" after laboring "for so long" as a pizza girl.

"Sounds fantastic," Jay responded sarcastically.

This time, he did not accompany her to New York.

While she was gone, he snooped through what few things she had accumulated since moving back. He found an old Vodafone bill from when she was living in London, and noticed the cell number was registered under the name Fritz Vandeveld.

"Son of a bitch," he said aloud. He tried not to mention anything until she returned, but when she called he was noticeably perturbed.

"Jay?" she whispered, as if she did not want to be heard.

"What?" he replied indignantly.

"I miss you. And I hate shooting birds. It's so boring."

"I don't know what to tell you, Mad."

"If I get on an earlier flight, do you want to meet me in New York?"

Jay paused. Normally, she would never even have to ask, but the context had changed.

"Jay?"

"Is he there with you?"

"Who?"

"You know who!"

This time Maddy paused. "I didn't know he would be here. He's a friend of Albert—"

"Tell the truth, Mad."

Silence followed.

"I can't talk about it right now. I will tell you everything. Meet me in New York. Please?"

Jay shook his head, exasperated by his own capitulation. "I fucking hate driving in New York." He exhaled audibly. "OK, I'll be at our usual spot when you land."

"Love you," she whispered. "I'll call you before I leave."

After he hung up, he buried his face in his hands.

Nervous about driving in the city alone, he hired a car to take him to the Carlyle Hotel. He abstained from grandiose gestures.

Maddy showed up on time and they went to Nobu for dinner.

"So tell me about the trip." At first, Jay was deliberately standoffish.

"It was awful. All those people are doing such amazing things with their lives, I felt like the biggest loser."

"If everyone compared themselves to lords and diplomats only the lords and diplomats would feel adequate."

"I know. But being there really made me miss you and Axl."

A half-smile crept onto Jay's lips. Quickly, he slammed a shot of Hakushika Tokusen sake and poured himself another from the clay carafe.

"So, tell me about your boyfriend."

Maddy rolled her eyes. "He's not my boyfriend."

As Maddy began her story, Jay continued pouring and shooting sake.

§   §   §

Felony charges of money laundering and tax evasion had been leveled against Fritz Vandeveld. Although he was not implicated as a conspirator in an international drug smuggling sting—at least not yet—his attorneys were concerned that it was only a matter of time before European Intelligence connected the dots. As soon as the allegations became public, his wife had filed for divorce, and the family had relinquished their support when it became clear that his name was under siege.

He was forced to resign from his position; his diplomat status was revoked, and many of his assets were frozen.

§ § §

Jay interjected, "Karma's a bitch!" He was numb from the rice wine but his thoughts were well lubricated. "But gahead, you have the floor."

§ § §

Around the same time Madison had arrived in Notting Hill, and unbeknownst to Desi, who was hoping to cultivate a romantic escapade of his own, Fritz and Maddy ended up living at Desi's together for the rest of that summer. Fritz purchased a cell phone plan for Maddy and paid for her dining and shopping expenses. They vacationed together and he gave her flying lessons on his private jet. Although he did not know Desmond personally, since Lord Albert was a mutual friend he was invited for a weekend holiday at Desi's château in the south of France. They showed up separately, and during tea Lord Albert "introduced" Maddy to Fritz.

Early on, it seemed realistic that Fritz would finally leave his wife, but as the summer progressed this possibility diminished. He began spending more time in Belgium with his children at their weekend cabin in Antwerp. Gradually, he was welcomed back into the family home. In tandem, Maddy grew despondent, and when Desi later learned of Fritz's presence at his flat he insisted she start paying rent. The night before she moved back home, Fritz reserved a room at the Heathrow Marriott. They slept in the same bed for the last time and promised to keep in touch.

When Maddy returned to London later that fall, she was expecting Fritz would meet her at the airport so they could drive to Lord Albert's together. Instead, Fritz sent a car. When she arrived at the Estate in Scarborough, he treated her as nothing more than a cordial acquaintance. Maddy was miserable and finally realized that Fritz would never go public with their relationship simply because she was an American girl with middle-class bloodlines.

§   §   §

Tears trickled down her cheeks as she finished speaking. Jay reached across the table and dabbed her face with his napkin.

"I can't believe I actually feel sorry for you."

"I know. I'm pathetic. I really am a loser."

"Don't say that."

"No. It's true." She gulped and her eyes grew watery again. "Do you know my first husband went on to run the M&A department at Goldman fucking Sachs." She sniffled quietly. "Look at me now. And I paid for his education." A few more tears trickled and Jay dabbed her face again. "You are the only person who has ever stood by me. I don't even know why you are still here."

"I don't know either," Jay said, but could not keep a straight face.

"Shut up." Maddy smiled back. "You're supposed to be consoling me."

When they got back to Lenox, their relationship reached its apex. After everything they had been through, Jay knew this would be their last chance. Maddy continued working at Ack's and at least for a while, she seemed genuinely appreciative of her life with Jay and Axl.

Almost every night, they dined out in Lenox or Great Barrington, and to the outside world they now classified themselves as "back together." Even the Gordon family admitted they noticed a positive change in her demeanor.

Two weeks before Thanksgiving, Jay surprised her with two tickets to St. Bart's. He hired a limo to take them to New York and they stayed at the Carlyle. For their first night, Jay had prepared another surprise.

It was a damp and raw Wednesday evening in early December and they were having drinks at Bemelman's bar, a classic Manhattan lounge inside the hotel. From the inside pocket of his blazer, Jay pulled out a robin's-egg blue box.

"Every girl should get a box from Tiffany's and you've never gotten one, so I wanted to be the first to give one to you."

He opened the box, revealing two dazzling diamond earrings. "And when you have children and your daughter is old enough to wear these earrings, I want you to tell her the story of the man in Bemelman's bar at the Carlyle Hotel who loves you so much."

Maddy was smiling and weeping and even Jay was teary. For nearly two full minutes thereafter, she was speechless. Finally, she placed her warm, moist cheek on the side of his neck and whispered into his ear, "You mean everything to me."

CHAPTER 40

The Highway Boys awake rested and refreshed. They eat a mammoth breakfast from the Marriott buffet and drink several cups of coffee. By eight-thirty they are back on the road. Jay cues up Whitesnake's "Here I Go Again On My Own," and Smitty counters with Journey's "Don't Stop Believing." For lunch, they dine in the outdoor courtyard at Frankie's in St. Louis, an Italian brasserie famous for its toasted raviolis. Jay ties Axl to a nearby tree and gives him a bowl of water. Afterwards, the waiter brings out a cart full of delectable pastries, gelatos and cakes. They each order homemade tiramisu and a cappuccino.

Jay takes this opportunity to acknowledge a past transgression. "So, while all that shit was going on with Maddy and the saga, I completely forgot you had called and I had spoken to you."

"It was quite a dick move, dude. But… at least now I know why."

"Well, actually there's more. When I realized I hadn't called you back and it had been like two months, I found Colin's number and called him because I suspected you were gonna tell me you had gotten engaged."

"Really? Colin was at the wedding and he never mentioned he spoke to you."

"But here's the good part: Colin told me when the wedding was and I wrote it down, but I was so fucked at the time, I lost the paper I wrote it on. Then when I was in St. Bart's I looked at a calendar in our room and thought the date looked familiar so I called my sister from the lobby of our hotel and had her check all the bridal shops and furniture stores in the greater San Diego area to see if there was a gift registry for the Walter Smith wedding. Sure enough, at Neiman Marcus, she found you."

Smitty is laughing and shaking his head sarcastically. "You son of a bitch. That's how you knew when to send the bouquet and those steak knives?"

"That's how I knew. And it's a good thing

I called when I did because the wedding was the next day!"

"That's pretty impressive, Jay. You're an all-star stalker."

"Uh, thanks, I think."

"That wasn't a compliment."

"Anyway dude, I'm sorry I missed the big day."

"You apologized three days ago. You are forgiven, again. So what happened when you got back from St. Bart's?"

CHAPTER 41

For people who grow up in the Northeast, the Caribbean in December is particularly magical, and Jay and Maddy were no exception. For the week, they were inseparable. During the days, they drank cocktails and played backgammon by the pool and chartered a yacht for trips around the island. After sunset they went skinny-dipping in the ocean, and at night they snuggled in their suite overlooking the beach.

On their last night in St. Bart's, Maddy put on an elegant Prada dress and wore her Tiffany earrings for the first time. Jay donned his white linen pants, a lilac linen shirt and a pair of John Lobb summer shoes. Before they left the room, Maddy said she wanted to phone her family. Jay let her have her privacy and he waited for her outside by the carport. She talked for almost forty minutes and when she finally came downstairs he could tell she had been crying. Having made dinner reservations at Maya's restaurant, they took a leisurely walk on Flammands beach.

"What's wrong?"

"I don't want to talk about it."

"Is everything OK at home?" In his heart, Jay knew she had not called her parents.

"Everything's fine," she replied in a shaky voice.

Jay shook his head. For the first time in months, that dark cloud of doubt loomed over him. He had a hard time eating and Maddy didn't even touch her dinner. He gazed at her earrings and kept telling himself that everything would work out if it was meant to be.

That night, Maddy slept with her back facing him and when Jay awoke in the morning, she was already showered and packed.

When they arrived at LaGuardia airport, it was dark and blisteringly cold. They took a cab back to the Carlyle, and when they got to the hotel Maddy excused herself to use the ladies room in Bemelman's Bar. They had not reserved a room and Jay was contemplating leaving the city that night. When Maddy emerged, she was gripping her cell phone and her demeanor was more cheerful.

"Do you want to stay in the city? I'm thinking we should just call a car and go back tonight," he said.

"Oh, OK sweetie."

"Yeah? You don't mind?"

"Oh no. Actually, I'm going to go hang out with Rachel. I feel bad because I still owe her money."

Jay's heart sank.

"But I'll see you at home."

"You don't want to come?"

"I do, but Rachel wanted to meet for drinks so I think I'll do that."

He nodded somberly.

"OK. Well at least let me put you in cab. It's freezing out there."

"Oh, thank you so much. You're so sweet."

Jay rolled her suitcase out on to the street and called for a taxi. Maddy got in and Jay shouted out Rachel's address. "Ninety-five Fifth Avenue, between ninth and tenth." He paid the driver in advance with a twenty-dollar bill.

Before Maddy got in, she kissed him on the lips. "Thank you for such a wonderful trip. And thank you of course for my amazing earrings."

"I'll see you up in the country."

As the car pulled away, Jay dashed into

the Carlyle and asked them to hold his bags behind the front desk. He tied a scarf around his neck and sprinted back outside, hailing a cab immediately.

"There's a Mazda MPV taxi about three blocks ahead of us; I need you to follow it. It's should be heading toward Fifth Avenue."

Sure enough, at a stoplight on East 72nd Street and Lexington Avenue, Jay spotted Maddy's taxi and could see her talking on her cell phone through the back window.

"Not too close," he instructed.

Both cabs continued south on Lexington, and when the yellow Mazda turned right onto East 63rd Street, Jay's cab followed. They crossed over Madison Avenue and made a left onto Fifth. Jay's heart was racing. Only two cars behind, he ducked when they paused at a light on East 61st Street. Once the light changed and motion resumed, he sat up and watched the cab ahead signal and pull over at East 55th Street.

"Stop right here!"

The cab veered to a halt and Jay handed the man a twenty-dollar bill.

"Just sit here for a minute."

Jay watched as Maddy got out of her cab and rolled her suitcase to the steps of the St. Regis hotel. A bellhop came out and escorted her luggage into the lobby. From his vantage,

Jay observed the silhouette of a tall man embrace her as she stepped indoors.

"Fuck me. Fuck me! Fuck me!"

"This is your wife?" the cab driver inquired in a Middle Eastern accent.

Jay was shaking. "Take me back to the Carlyle, please. Seventy-sixth and—"

He could not say the word Madison.

He checked into his usual room at the Carlyle and lay in bed fighting off the inevitable tears.

He called the St. Regis hotel and asked if they had a guest by the name of Fritz Vandeveld. The concierge acknowledged that Mr. Vandeveld had checked in earlier that evening.

"Would you like me to put you through to his room?"

"No, that's OK," Jay replied. "But what I would like to do is pay for his stay. I'll give you a credit card number. Can you take payment over the phone?"

The concierge hesitated.

"It's an early Christmas present."

Jay rattled off the numbers and expiration date of his AmEx and then gave the sternest instructions.

"When he goes to pay for the room, I want you to be sure to tell him that it has been taken care of by Mr. Jay Gordon."

The concierge said he would leave explicit instructions for whomever handled checkout for the Diplomat suite.

"Thank you." Jay hung up and put on his coat, gloves and scarf. He needed to take a walk. The night stung, and as he strolled he exhaled clouds of steam. His adrenaline was still speeding, which softened the bitter wind. He walked all night, trying to gather his thoughts and gain some perspective. By sunrise, his fingers and toes were frozen and his cheeks were raw and rosy. Without sleeping, he called the car service and checked out of the hotel. On the drive back to the Berkshires, he lay slumped over in the backseat of a Lincoln Town Car, mentally and emotionally drained.

CHAPTER 42

"Holy shit." It is nighttime on Interstate 70 and Smitty is behind the wheel. "That's a fucking horrible story."

Jay has been talking for over three hours and the mood in the Range Rover is somber—and sober.

"Yup. Like Boca Josh always used to say, that girl was a lemon. Beautiful exterior, great body, fun to be with but always broke down. And just never worked."

Smitty concurs. "That pretty much sums it up."

"Yeah, Boca's always been on top of his metaphors."

"So that's it? That's the end?"

"Well, not really, but that's where I offi-

317

cially made my exodus. But there is one more thing I need to tell you about."

Smitty is pessimistic. "Oh, no. What now?"

"It's not like that. Pull over so I can drive and you can roll us a joint."

Using the much-maligned road atlas, Smitty rolls an enormous cone while Jay cues up Aerosmith's seminal ballad "Angel."

§ § §

In 1984, Jay developed a crush on a girl named Chloe Vastir. They were both eighth graders at Berkshire Country Day, and before graduation that spring he noticed blossoming breasts under her low-cut blouse. Boca Josh, who grew up in the Berkshires before attending boarding school in Montreal, asked Chloe out on behalf of Jay. She accepted. Their date was at the Pittsfield Cinema Center, where they watched *Footloose* and held hands in their seats. Later that night, they kissed awkwardly and Jay touched her breasts. However, things had moved too rapidly for Chloe, so the next day Boca received a phone call from Valerie Vastir, Chloe's older sister, who informed him that Jay and Chloe were no longer together.

That fall, Jay went off to boarding school

with a chip on his shoulder and a picture of his "ex-girlfriend."

§   §   §

"Wait a second." Smitty lights the spliff and takes two long pulls. "Is this the same girl you were tossing off to when I met you junior year?"

Jay chuckled. "The very same girl. Throughout high school, I kept thinking about those cute little boobies."

Smitty passed the joint. "Outstanding!"

§   §   §

Four years later, Jay returned from Mount Hermon Academy with a big ego and boarding school party habits. Having not gone to high school locally, he knew virtually no one in the area. It was summertime so he borrowed his parents Jeep Wrangler soft-top convertible and drove to the Cinema Center to watch Tim Burton's *Batman* on the big screen. As he was inching through the parking lot, "Paradise City" blaring from his speakers, he spotted four girls who waved to him.

Jay slowed down, raised his shoulders and tilted his head to the right with extreme machismo bravado. As he got closer, he recognized that two of the girls were Chloe and Valerie Vastir. It turned out that they were also going to see *Batman* and they invited him to come along.

"Screw *Batman*. I got a fake ID. Let's go get drunk by the lake."

Valerie and her two friends followed, and Chloe rode with Jay. Stopping first at the package store, Jay bought a bottle of Gordon's gin. Outside in the parking lot, he leaned into Valerie's car and proudly flashed the liquor. "See this ladies, Gordon's gin for Mr. Gordon." They girls giggled almost mockingly but in his mind, he was John Bender from *The Breakfast Club*. They all proceeded to Stockbridge Bowl. After a few plastic cups of gin and guava juice, Jay and Chloe wandered off alone.

Under the moon glow they began kissing and petting. Jay reached under her shirt, but just before he groped her breasts, he paused.

"So, you gonna break up with me if I touch your boobs again?"

Although they never had sex, this turned into a hot summer romance. However, by the end of August, they were both headed to college. Chloe left for Dartmouth, and a week later Jay went to Cornell. Within two months, they lost touch.

Seventeen years later, Jay had just moved out of the house he'd lived in with Maddy and was busy trying to franchise Ack's Pizza Shack. On a random weekday afternoon, he got a text message from his sister in San Francisco. The message read: *I had a dream you married Chloe Vastir*

Jay had grown somewhat superstitious over the years, and when he got home he Googled Chloe and found a plethora of information, including her business email address.

A former corporate executive at Sun Microsystems, she was now the sole proprietor of a thoroughbred equestrian training school, which she ran out of Aspen, Colorado. Jay sent her a short email with the subject header: *Blast from the past*. She responded within hours.

They corresponded via email for a few weeks and she was flabbergasted to learn that the same "bad-ass kid" had opened three successful restaurants in their hometown. They began speaking casually on the phone and eventually she unraveled a complicated saga involving a bipolar, codependent ex-boyfriend. He assured her that if *anyone* could relate, it would be him.

A month later, she flew home to attend the wedding of one of her sister's high school friends. Jay and Chloe had dinner at Maison.

Over the course of the weekend he told her about a relationship saga of his own.

Without any romantic advances, a discernible spark had been ignited. In a phone conversation with Boca Josh, he described Chloe as "the antithesis of Madison Horn."

Twice a month he flew to Colorado to spend the weekend with her. As a prominent figure within the local business community, she helped Jay establish relationships with restaurateurs and commercial leasing agents. They had sex for the first time the night before Ack's Pizza Shack opened in Aspen.

§ § §

"Whoa!" Smitty is taken aback. "Wait a second! You own a restaurant in Aspen?"

Jay is beaming.

"Look at you, dude. I haven't seen a shit-eating grin that large since we were sucking back boomers in Chapman House!"

"You ready for the punchline?" Jay grips the wheel of the Range Rover loosely, as cruise control has taken over.

"What the fuck is going on?"

"I'm getting married!"

"What?"

"I'm getting married. Saturday morning. You are my best man."

"Don't fuck with me!"

"I'm dead serious, Smit."

"Well what about my—"

"It's been taken care of. Your wife is waiting for us in Colorado. The boys from Chapman will be there. This, my friend, is the fucking bachelor party."

"Dude, what the fuck?" Smitty is too shocked to be hostile.

"I had to do it like this. After my performance when you got married, or lack thereof, I knew you would resent getting an invitation in the mail."

"And what makes you think I don't resent this?"

"Well, I figured I'd get you fucked up on a road trip, give you my heart-wrenching explanation of why I missed *your* wedding, and all that would soften the news."

"It's the old surprise-the-best-man-with-a-wedding-announcement road-trip. Strong move, Gordy. That's a real strong move!" Smitty shakes his head.

"Thanks. I've been planning this for months."

"Now if I only had a bottle of bubbly underneath my seat."

"We don't need bubbly. Pop open the glove."

Smitty unlatches the glove compartment,

reaches around and pulls out a small wooden humidifier with two Jean Jarreau Arawak cigars.

He nearly chokes when he sees the engraving on the box. "I'm fucking speechless."

"The wedding itself is going to be pretty low-key, so I thought we might have to celebrate with a little style beforehand."

"We're still going to a strip club, right?"

They approach the Oklahoma City Center exit and Jay flips on his turning signal and glares at Smitty incredulously.

"I'm joking," Smitty jabs. "But we should at least go to Hooters. I mean, we're in Oklahoma for God's sake. And this is a bachelor party."

"That's actually a pretty solid idea."

"You're fuckin' right it's a solid idea. Big bucket o' wings, a few pitchers of Bud and a flock of corn-fed blondes. What's not to like?"

Jay laughs and sticks out his fist. Smitty returns with a pound.

"Congratulations, bro. Seriously."

"Thanks, man."

CHAPTER 43

Madison was at the check-out desk at the St. Regis hotel when she heard the concierge inform Fritz that a Mr. Gordon had paid for his room. Her face turned red and she slithered away, pretending she hadn't heard. Without citing a reason, Fritz promptly cancelled their shopping lunch at Barney's and hired a car to take her back to Massachusetts. Maddy held her composure until they parted company, but once she was alone, her emotions spilled over.

Hours later, she was, yet again, on her parents' doorstep. Her face was still golden from a week in St. Bart's, yet her puffy eyes and dried tears dulled the luster of a healthy tan. She noticed her boxes lined up against the garage, as Jay had come by to unload the rest of her belongings. Almost metaphorically, rain clouds loomed in the horizon.

Maddy mustered the strength to heave all of her items inside. When she was finished, she froze in her tracks as something in the corner of the garage caught her eye. Collapsed on its side, covered in dust and buried under a box of spilled tools, she spotted the handgrips on her old mountain bike. She smiled with the zeal of a teenager and prodded the clutter until the bike was freed. She found an old sweatshirt and wiped it off, sprayed the chain with WD-40 and adjusted the seat.

Dark winter clouds blanketed the heavens as she wheeled the bike out of the garage and onto the cracked blacktop driveway. She was still wearing the custom-made Domenico Vacca suit Jay had bought for her. She mounted and pedaled onto the street, a feeling of youthfulness overtaking her, as if no time had passed between excursions. She pedaled by the old Faith First complex. A freezing January gust rustled through the barren trees. She pedaled to the end of her block, gathering momentum and reveling in rare spontaneity. Exhaling deep breaths, she continued on toward Lenox proper. Icy droplets of rain pelted the pavement in sporadic intervals. The sky was ominous but Maddy was blissful as she sped along. She zipped passed the candy store on Church Street and then on to Maison. She noticed Jay's silver Audi in the parking lot and kept right on pedaling. She turned left on the corner and coasted down Bolt Way, passing Ack's on the right. She kept going. The horizontal hail intensified and the charcoal sky was both empty and menacing. She pedaled fast on inclines and stood tall on downward slopes, letting her hair flutter and freeze. Her suit was now damaged but she was in no hurry to stop riding or seek shelter.

Knowing Jay was at the restaurant, she decided to go visit Axl. When she got to the house, the front door was locked, so she tapped the bell repeatedly and kept calling for her dog. After a while, Axl appeared in the door, and when he saw her he trotted back into the kitchen nonchalantly. This deflated Maddy's euphoria. She now felt her cold, wet clothes clinging to her skin. It was time to go home. A part of her felt distressed at having ruined a $4,000 custom suit but she was happy to have rediscovered simplistic, bygone exuberance. Battling the elements, she pedaled slowly as the feeling of loneliness grew suffocating. Her cheeks ached and her hair clumped together like Popsicle dreadlocks.

When she arrived at home, she found Jane in a darkened dining room, staring out at the backyard through the window. She trudged upstairs and peeled off her clothes, tying a bathrobe around her waist and limping back down to the family sofa. She did not bother to turn on the lights. In the midst of it all, she sensed her life was changing yet again. She had worn out every relationship and every experience, and was left with only memories, more painful than comforting.

Outside, the rain pelted against the rooftop in a rhythmic belligerence and with a chilling reverberation, as if the wind cried Maddy.

CHAPTER 44

The orange molten embers of two cigar tips glow inside the Range Rover. Along with the musky gusts of Arawak tobacco, a content quiet pervades the air. Axl keenly smacks his mouth as he digests a small plate of barbecued pulled pork. A pair of freshly creased "HOOTERS – Oklahoma City" T-shirts are draped from the rear seat headrest. Behind the wheel, Jay cracks his window and a stagnant smoke cloud rushes toward the open breeze. Smitty taps his index finger on his cigar and a perfect ring of ash cascades into the open ashtray. The highway is dark and desolate.

After a few miles, Smitty shatters the calm with his usual jostling banter. "So Jay Gordon's buying the freakin' cow! And they said it would never happen."

Jay smiles. "Who's they?"

"They, my friend, is the figurative entity representing the doubt that many of us who've known you all these years have expressed at one time or another."

"I didn't know it was like that."

"Well... it *was*." Smitty takes a long draw from his cigar. "What's surprising is that you haven't really 'known' this chick for that long."

Jay flashes Smitty a don't-call-my-fiancée-a-chick look. "Well, considering I knew her in grade school, I wouldn't say that."

"But usually you put all your women through the four-year, Jay Gordon relationship training program."

Jay chuckles. "Apparently my reputation precedes me."

Smitty scratches his scruff. "Let's see, there was your on-again-off-again college girl. I know I'm not supposed to mention her name, but I figure since you're tying the knot, it's water under the bridge now. She was, what, four years?"

"Give or take."

"OK. Then the chick from UMass."

"Another four."

"Then, the most recent lunatic, whose name I refuse to mention."

"Yeah. That wasn't quite four years, but it felt like twenty."

Smitty sniffs the stub of his cigar. "Fucking fantastic stogie, by the way."

Jay responds by bellowing out a long puff.

"So, the question is: How long have you actually been with your future wife?"

"Well, this was unlike any other relationship I've ever had. We were old friends. And in an adolescent sort of way, she was my ex."

"I remember the picture on your desk at Chapman," Smitty interjects.

"Exactly! That was Chloe. So then we became new/old friends and we stared emailing and IMing and then texting. Then we started making plans to hang out. I would visit her in Colorado. She came back to Lenox a few times."

"Her folks still live there, right?"

"They do. But she stayed with me." Jay gives his friend a quick wink. "One thing led to another and we began sleeping together. But everything was super-casual. We never talked about being boyfriend/girlfriend or anything like that."

"No terms?" Smitty peels off the ring around the Arawak before tossing its remains out the window. "That's unlike you."

"Yeah, it was. But I already did the whole textbook fairy tale, buy the girl Tiffany's, drink champagne on a chartered plane romance. Chloe isn't like that."

"So, how'd you pop the question?"

"It's not much of a story. One morning, we were lying in bed. Things were going really well. We had just had sex. I looked at her and said, 'We should get married.' It felt completely right, yet totally spontaneous. She was like, 'I do' and then we had sex again and went to brunch."

"Awesome."

"Every fucking engagement story should go exactly like that."

They laugh.

"I mean, we're in our mid-thirties."

"Yup," Smitty concurs. "Why beat around the bush?"

"Indeed."

"Speaking of bushes," Smitty announces, "I could sure use a toke of some of that fine Canadian shrubbery."

Jay pops open the console and pulls out his glass one-hitter. "Pack it."

"OK, but can you pull over first so I can say goodnight to the missus."

"What's the matter there, Clyde," Jay jousts in an ingratiating tone, "can't talk to wifey after a little hit of the reef?"

"No, actually, I can't. She will know. I will get shit for it. Just wait till you're married. They develop a sixth sense, you'll see."

"I don't think so, Smit. Not only does Chloe smoke, she keeps a little jar stashed in her thong drawer. Good shit, too."

Smitty's jaw plummets. "Are you fucking kidding me? This broad sounds like a winner!"

"Broad, now? What are you, Andrew Dice Clay? Show some respect."

"You know what I mean."

Jay slows down and flips on his turning signal, pointing to the rest area.

"For what?" Smitty protests.

"Don't you have to make a *phone call*?"

"Can't you find a gas station or something? There's no people and no light."

Jay rolls his eyes. "Don't be a pansy."

"Dude, I take it you haven't seen *The Hitcher.*"

"Uh, no." Jay waves the pipe. "Just make your call so we can fire this bitch up."

"Fine, but keep the headlights on and honk the horn if I start pacing."

As the car crawls to a stop, Smitty exits. Jay motors down the passenger side window and calls out into the night, "Oh, by the way, you can mention the wedding! Your wife knows all about it!"

Smitty's cell phone is pressed against his ear and he gives Jay a thumbs-up.

Jay takes this moment alone to send Chloe a text message. Then he leans into the backseat to scratch behind Axl's ears. After a few minutes, he glances up and notices Smitty wandering into the distance. With a twinkle, he taps his horn a few times. Moments later, Smitty appears in the headlight beams jabbering away. In a fluid, snapping motion, he flips his cell phone shut, stuffs it into his pocket and climbs into the car.

"Lara's all excited about this wedding. I gotta hand it to you, buddy, you planned this thing pretty well and still managed to shock the piss out of me."

Jay sticks out his fist and Smitty taps it.

"You ready to get this show on the road?" Jay hands Smitty the pipe.

"Green hit. Sweet. I will do the honors." Smitty clears his throat. "Here's to you and yours, and to mine and ours, and if mine and ours ever come across you and yours, I hope you and yours will do as much for mine and ours as mine and ours have done for you and yours."

"Amen."

Checking his side mirrors, Jay accelerates and veers abruptly to the left, the tires spinning and kicking up dust. As the Range Rover careens towards the entrance ramp, all three passengers bounce from the momentum but settle comfortably as cruising speed is restored. Subtly he flips through his iPod and lands on Bon Jovi's "Wanted Dead or Alive."

As the song begins, he pumps up the volume and guides the steering wheel with his knees so he can harness his air guitar and gracefully tingle his fingers in synch with Richie Sambora's soft strings. Smitty smirks audaciously as he exhales.

"It's all the same, only the names will change..." Jay fervently mouths the words. Axl scratches his neck, rattling his collar with his hind paw. Jay grips the iPod like a microphone and belts out the rest of the verse. Smitty joins in. Once again, the open road swallows the Highway Boys as they continue to motor westward.